The Town

The Town

BP Gregory

2nd Edition

Thank you to my beloved husband without whom this story would not have seen the light.

Copyright © 2023 BP Gregory

ISBN-13 978 0 6457319 6 5

This is the second edition, published 2023. The first edition was published 2017.

ACKNOWLEDGMENTS

The Town cover images are by Pavelr and Tim Bird; Flora & Jim cover image by Marcel Jancovic; Orotund cover image by Alex Malikov; and Visit the Website image by Peter Dedeurwaerder, all courtesy of Shutterstock.

Sensitivity reading for Aboriginal content provided courtesy of Angie Faye Martin of Versed Writings. For more information visit versedwritings.com.

Once again it's thankyou to my amazing team of proof readers: Ahren Morris the Cunning, Nola James the Intrepid, Jason Steen the Bold, Diane Gregory the Meticulous, and St Martin in the Paddocks. Your love and the lengths you'll travel to help are astounding and humbling to me every day.

CONTENT ADVISORY

This story features adult themes including addiction: alcoholism, animal violence, bushfires including loss of property and life, bullying, mental health issues, and traumatic death.
It references the testing of harmful substances on people without their informed consent. It references institutional abuse. It references the forcible removal of Aboriginal and Torres Strait Islander people from their families and country.
It may not be suitable for all readers.

The author lives on Wurundjeri country would like to acknowledge the Aboriginal and Torres Strait Islander people of Australia, the traditional custodians of the land, waterways and sky; their strength of culture and their enduring connection to country. The author pays her respects to their Elders past, present, and emerging.

TABLE OF CONTENTS

CHAPTER ONE

BURNOUT

Astounded and wobbly sick, instead of raising the alarm Kate sleepwalked through the rest of her shift and then took herself home.

The heavy *clack* and thick miasma as she opened her front door no longer nauseated. Neither did the linen middens she had to high step over; even the crockery fermenting in the sink was comforting. Her habits were sculpting a modest landscape, a safe crack to hide in where she was destined to moulder quietly and become one with the carpet.

Shopping bags rattled. Sod the rest, the bottle of wine vanished, Kate cannonballed it. Migrating restlessly room to room with her glass to leave new burgundy circles as though re-marking territory. "Beating the bounds," it used to be called.

She caromed off sweaty walls and with low cunning left the lamps dark as evening dug in, denying what had been witnessed. Denying she could see at all. So far as tactics went it only congealed both the humidity and her anxiety, a pinch of cornstarch to the air.

Finally Kate capitulated. She coiled up in the lounge's debris, a python bloated with all she had no wish to know, and dialled her supervisor. A confidante would have been better but she had nobody else to tell. Took him long enough to pick up.

'It's Kate.' Twisting the stem of her empty glass fitfully, already longing for more. Which was as sober Kate had predicted: that drunk Kate would get too smeary too quick to go back out. Not that anyone would sell to her in that state. Look at her, already having to grip the couch to stay propped. Smug sober Kate needed a slap. 'I reviewed the material.'

Supervisor Gary made polite sounds to cover disinterest, because that was his job. 'Kate, hi. Wow. You're through the stack already?' It had been busy-work, the sort you dump on interns for long tedious hours to make them question squandering those university big bucks. 'Is there some kind of problem?'

The line was so clear Kate could hear the idiot box squeal excitedly in the background, and knew Gary would be swivelled to fix an eye on it. Dinner interrupted, steaming on the coffee table. And every light blazing. Drive out the edges, the risk, the sullen grey.

She bit lightly at her glass. 'You bet your ass in slacks there's a problem.'

He sighed. *Here we go*. 'Kate …'

'I found an anomaly. Where the burn's been through, I saw it on the composite image.' Mouth stained she was already numbling the words. Hammer descending to bludgeon her out of her misery. 'It looks like a town.'

'Hang on.'

A clatter. The volume of the program's chipper squeaking came down like a hand clapped over a mouth. Their connection became so quiet that Kate could make out an aggressive hiss to the signal, had to hold it away from her head.

It was the sound of all that light storming through from his cosy home. If she were willing to get up she could scissor open the blinds and see it for herself out there in the urban distance; a star radiant in darkness. Instead she squeezed her eyes shut and her own grimy walls commenced swing dancing.

Supervisor Gary graced her with his return. 'Kate, you're mistaken. You have to be. There's nothing out there.'

Red rag to a bull. 'Well there isn't any more, *Gary*! I've got the images spread across my kitchen bench right now. The fire front gutted it.'

'Honestly Kate, how often do we have to go through this? You can't be taking confidential material home.'

'Seriously? What if there were people? A bushfire like that, they couldn't have got out! They wouldn't have stood a chance!'

'Ah, jeeze—you're crying, aren't you? Please, please stop.' He would be squinting at the clock, hung in a showroom kitchen where light twinkled off every surface. 'Are you drunk Kate, is that it?'

'I'm not crying! For fuck's sake!'

But she was. Had to poke herself in the face to realise.

The damp misty cloud that surrounded Kate, that she was sunk in, where all was grey, grey, grey, stirred curiously. It *knew* crying. Understood the gesture but was having trouble coupling it to emotion. Was her body being sad without her?

In her mind Kate privately called the deadening grey phenomenon the seep, because folk love using fancy names to claim things solely as their own.

The seep was a curtain that dropped. A thickening, a floundering between her and the world. So real, to Kate at least, that even in this heat she could feel water droplets beading on her cheeks. The seep arrived in its own time but could be more reliably poured from a bottle.

She touched her confounding tears. A town. A whole town. Nobody would have stood a chance.

Supervisor Gary was droning on in her ears but the hiss of light burgeoned nastily over him as though she had stepped on its nest. Assaulting ears rather than eyes, viciously biting her face until she gave up and terminated the call.

Silence. That was better, in the smothering suck of her thoughts.

As Kate lay there the wet caul of alcohol slowed even them. Slowed. Until all was quiet and dark.

CHAPTER TWO

OCCUPIED

The humidity stubbornly failed to break the next day, squelching wilted optimism that had hoped *it'll all be better come morning*. The mantra of the trapped. Only idiots thought like that anymore.

The dawn commute became a jostling sweaty killer. By quarter past eight the corporate washroom was packed solid by crumpled wage slaves and couriers, sink-baths shoulder to shoulder. It was like visiting a safari waterhole.

Hell for anyone who might be hiding out in a cubicle after a rough night, just trying to shift a post-binge brick in peace.

By nine fifteen they all bustled away and it was safe for Kate to emerge. The ruin they left behind looked like the apocalypse had been. Every scrap of toilet paper and towel had been soiled, spilling and looping from the trashcan. The mirrors wore enough makeup to start their own TV show. The cleaners were going to weep.

The clattering office was the same as always, which Kate found eerie. As though nothing of note had been uncovered yesterday, nothing changed. Possibly the stupefying air was to blame: the cheap institutional carpet smell had to be rinsed from her hair and clothes at the end of each day so as not to spread it about at home and spoil what she had brewing there.

Kate perched in Gary's guest chair and swivelled, with lazy sweeps of her legs, to make the bearings scream. Back, *pause*, and forth. Mainly because it ought to drive him bonkers, it would drive any sane soul bonkers.

But Gary never tipped over the edge. Just kept glancing with long-suffering martyrdom at the framed portrait of his family, his daughter's crappy sketches of sunbeams. *Give me strength*, Gary's tight lips implored.

And apparently they did, which was novel. Most succumbed to management as a last ditch effort to get away from home life. Easier to think of sunbeams and portraits from a distance and pretend to love them more.

'It's not like I'm saying you're *wrong*, Kate. I'm not saying that. But no-one has been able to verify what you say you saw.'

'What I "say."'

Not a whisker out of place in his sincerity, like supervision was something he'd studied in acting school.

Kate had woken with an inflamed brain to scour her flat top to bottom. The images she had poured over last night were gone. Not even a trace, which sent her into an inconsolable rage at drunk Kate. Or was there a chance somebody had been in her rooms?

Kate's neighbours were nameless sardines packed on all sides, their lives transmitting in queer ways through the building. She scarcely recalled those early days when she had first moved in: bleary exhaustion from bolting awake at every whimper or bang. That level of terror alert could not be sustained. Nowadays an intruder could probably clomp to her bed and poke a finger right up her nose.

Still, Kate's native habitat was easy territory to get lost in, beginning to resemble a prime time episode of *When Hoarders Attack*. A little early to be blaming, yet, a little late to be leaving for work. So she had hurried out the door, only to find that printing a fresh copy was not on the cards either.

What are you talking about? the computer queried innocently, tempting her to put her fist through its sly screen. Those same codes that had unearthed the town now returned a bird's eye view of trees, trees and more trees. A swathe of blackened ash right through the middle that no services had scrambled to save because there was nothing out there. There never had been.

But there had. Drunk Kate knew it for sure, stirring deep down in the depths where she was lurking.

'So give me something to work with, then. Get me some proof.' That was how things worked in Garyland: nice, clean cut and simple, like popping to the shops.

At least he had the grace not to mention her blubbering down the phone. The expectation it would not happen again could remain just as elegantly unsaid.

Kate returned to her foxhole numbly. Acutely aware in the bustle how everyone around her had an actual job to do, burrowed into it like ticks. Not that she needed a single one of these assmonkeys to believe her claim.

The break room boasted a corkboard where between charity raffles staff could tack up screenshots of weird shit. Configurations resembling a cock and balls were predictably popular. It was a shrine to imaging software hiccups and humanity's hardwired desperation to see meaning in anything.

Picking up the phone to the council failed to yield gold. 'Honey, I'm not sure what to tell you except there's no town there. Sure you're not getting your sites skewiff?'

The list stretched long, but there were few things Kate loathed more than pet names from strangers. 'Is there anything nearby?'

'According to these files, state sponsored a kind of research institute for a while, the Pillars Institute, but it's been long closed. More's the pity the fire didn't go there—would have saved a tidy heap in maintenance.'

Long deep breaths, Kate. Gritting her teeth, because people rarely realised how utterly infuriating they were. Oh sure, a boxy government installation and an orderly constellation of residences could look so similar. Not worth getting in a flap over.

The hot barb of curiosity up her ass would not let her sit still. *Did* she know what she saw? Suspicious that drunk Kate knew more than she was letting on, crucial memory sluiced away by wine.

So. Kate gnawed the end of her pen: perhaps she was going about this wrong. If there were people out there in the bush what did they need? Not to be happy, of course, that preposterous shining grail; but let's say just to exist. To successfully turn the days over like cards, one at a time.

Kate ran her mind back over her own day. Was it clean water? Power? A sewage system that did not leak into the loungeroom? These were all luxuries hoarded by a smirking fraction of the world's population ... but having had them, folk would probably be loathe to go without.

Kate got nothing from the utility providers, after painful hours of looped hold music that burned up the day, *nothing.* The mysterious town and whoever it sheltered seemed to have been off the grid. Unusual but certainly not impossible.

The mystery nagged at her. *What did people need?* Answers, Kate insisted silently. The pillbox fan on her desk whirred in time to her beating thoughts. People need answers.

The fire station local to the suspect area was her next obvious port of call. Never mind that if their duty officer had noticed anything amiss it would be the firemen raising hell right now, not some paranoid woman from an office in the city.

Her call was snatched up on the first ring. 'Yes, hello?' His greeting a peculiar mix of eagerness and caution because there was no such thing as a good fire. Even limiting things to property damage was nothing to celebrate: the loss could ruin people, and hard. Then there were the screaming burns that would not cool. Flesh that cracked and hardened.

Bursting with life, though, this lad on the phone. Still thought himself the big man. Exhausting. Even worse, he laughed at Kate and she nearly bit through her tongue in anger. 'Wouldn't you think we'd know? It's a big slice out of the ass end of bumfuck out there, I'll give you that, but we were monitoring that burn pretty good. Doesn't take much before charring a couple of hectares of bush nobody cares about becomes knocking right at your front door.'

Kate slammed the handset in the cradle before it dawned that the fireman may not have been laughing maliciously. Some idiots were naturally cheerful. Oh well. She refused to dwell on rudeness to a stranger she was never going to see again.

With a sudden crack and puff of scorched wiring, her fan fell into pieces which skittered away across the desk. At the same time her phone shrilled. Had she been wound tight instead of melting in the heat she would have shrieked.

'Kate here.'

The surrounding hum of the cubicle farm sank away. 'You sound quite the intriguing lady there, *Kate*.'

The brash young fireman's voice was lower this time, unwelcomely intimate. Dead air hissed behind him, a boiling inferno. Kate slapped the phone back down with reflexive revulsion as though a leech had slid into her ear.

Her pulse stuttered. Anxious as though he had followed her somehow, a swift and grinning arrow even now peering in at her window. But anger flushed that out pretty fast. This was a grownup world where adults were trying to work, not some tween meat market.

She nudged the phone off the hook as she scooped together her notes. Overcame her revulsion long enough to scrape the fan's remnants into the bin where they twitched, feeble, dying.

'Kate?' The receptionist warbled her name, standing up like a forest lemur to project. Shouting was the accepted medium for overcoming cubicle walls, and if you could not drill through you went over the top.

Kate clenched her fists. 'The answer is no.'

'But he sounds cuuuute, *and* he's a fireman!'

'He's not charming, and he'll carry on with that wrong assumption until the day somebody tazes him.' That shut her up, but by now Kate had scratchy chitin legs running up and down her spine. The fireman might be harmless. The town might be no more than the ethanol goblins come knocking. She was not about to put money on either.

The IT team were supposed to be stopping by to check her terminal for deleted, dropped or clandestinely altered data; given their funding however, Kate decided she would be better off waiting for Christmas. She finished packing and checked out, throwing the sulking secretary a kiss in exchange for a well earned middle finger.

It was still miserably hot out, the air something Kate wanted to scrape off her skin in great jellied handfuls. Joining the crowd was calming, though. *En mass* humanity provided the best place to be alone.

The couple who ran the food store on Kate's way home thought they knew her habits. They were so pleased to recommend this or that wine that had just swooped through the door and chat about its provenance, their weekend away to patronise the vineyard.

Kate smiled where appropriate and weathered it. Her only consideration was price point, caring just enough about their opinion to not want to appear a cheap drunk. And only one bottle at a time, never by the case no matter how they tried to tempt her. That way might as well be marked Here Be Fucking Dragons. To drunk Kate each glass was a task to be resolved as quickly as possible.

Home again. Home was where the heart was—or at least enough shed skin cells to make a whole other Kate lurking in the dark corners. She stamped the bottle on the bench like a marker.

Then took out a felt tipped pen and sketched what she remembered of the burnt site, the town, around it. Drew directly onto the benchtop, a nice little piece of geography right there in her home. Try losing *this*.

Even charred to a cinder it had definitely been a town. A person would have to be some kind of asshole to mistake it for anything else, to laugh airily and claim, 'Oh it's nothing,' so they could go back to swilling their horseshit coffee and watching their programs. If it were important it would be on the news already, right, so why be uptight?

The wine was all plummy darkness poured into her. Matched her irritation. The liquor itself was a distillation of place, of vineyards and philosophies; and exposure to places changed you. Exposure to wine dramatically changed Kate: sober Kate to drunk Kate, neither of whom could fully trust or understand the other.

She sipped steadily, on a mission, orbiting her new drawing. A dark cloud herself, she tried to draw the seep back around her feelings, missing its comforting blankness.

But the town had disturbed the weather. Her responsibility, bringing it here, integrating it into the contained world she had been nurturing. Especially as the damned place had been rejected from reality once already, vanishing overnight while she snored on the sticky loungeroom floor.

Did the citizens of her miniature town now gape up from the bench at her towering features, etched in threatening cumulus? A biblical crimson flood looming from a wineglass the size of the moon? A whimsy, that thought, but it churned ice through her intestines nonetheless.

Kate was disturbed enough to compulsively lock, unlock, then relock the front door. *To be safe*, she told herself, patting it. *Just being sensible.* Catching herself going back ten seconds later to do it again she had to admit that if she wanted to still have fingernails come morning, perhaps tonight was not the best night to be alone.

Hesitant to pick up the phone. Hand overing over it while her aggrieved eyes went wide, black and feline. Which was stupid. It was hardly going to bite, or explode sending sharp plastic everywhere. She resolutely dialled the agency. Bless all hours service, her guy, which was how she liked to think of him, was available.

Kate's guy's name was Gary, like her supervisor. It had provoked enough of a chuckle to pick him from the catalogue. No thousand ships getting launched by his headshot but at least to her his eyes had seemed kind. He could be Tradesman Gary, or Visiting Colleague Gary. Hardly the sort to set the landings clucking *ooh a rent boy!* as he came and went.

Rent Boy Gary's first words as he tramped through the front door were, 'Oh no, you didn't need to tidy for me, really.'

Which was what you got for judging a book by its cover. Her guy's eyes may be kind but his mouth not so much. Still, the sting of outrage aside Kate had warmed to his blunt cheer pretty quickly, the opposite of Supervisor Gary in every way. He was like the anti-Gary. 'I wasn't aware I'd rung Renovator Rescue. Although I have phoned every bloody one else today, so why not?'

Gary sniggered and poured himself a glass without asking. Hardly a guest; orienting in others' spaces was a natural outthrust of his work. 'Looks like some kindling and one good match would solve all your problems.'

He might have been flirting—hard to tell sometimes—but the whole problem going up in flames was a literal solution of sorts. *Knocking right at your front door*. She shuddered inside her skin.

And there he went, flipping on lights and opening windows. Stirring the gloom of her tawdry nest. 'You need to take better care of yourself, Kate.'

'Why?'

That stymied her guy. Gary stood with his head on one side for a bit, then drained his purloined drink, a snap like a lizard gulping a mouse. 'Because this is all there is, dumbass. All there's going to be. Might as well make the best of it. Speaking of, mind if I smoke?'

What a question. The raspy crumbling whiff was repulsive, but everything in here was already repulsive. What harm could Gary do with his pink mouth and loose easy way?

He leaned against the wall and Kate had to concede he looked more at home with leaking cigarette and bottomless wineglass jammed in the same gesticulating hand. More like his glamour shot. How he managed drinking without putting out an eye, now *there* was a life skill.

'Something's eating you.' The statement grinding in lungs

already phlegmy. Perhaps the Big C gnawing away in there waiting to carry her guy off. 'Thought that's what you hired me for. Anything to confess?'

That made Kate laugh her best laugh, brash and window rattling. 'Confess? At your rates?'

'Off the clock. Scout's honour.'

Not difficult to comprehend the loyalty of his client base. Gary hawked the chance to pretend somebody gave a shit, even a little, and it was heady stuff. Lonely folk shelling out to tell themselves fairytales in the dark. The biggest of all was of course that they would be remembered, pass on but leave some kind of shape in the world.

'Fine.' Kate rubbed her brow, weighed her phrasing. 'I've been thinking. What do people need?'

'Basic hygiene.'

'I'm serious.'

'So am I. Health is at the top of the list.' Illustrated with a drag that went right down to his toes, and a plume she tried not to retch from. Hot and full of cinders. It was not *her* seep.

Garry tapped his ash neatly out the window. 'Um. You've also got l'amour. Figure that's a nice easy one, business is always booming. And I guess … something to believe in. Purpose, you know? A direction to march when you get up of a morning.'

'Huh. That's pretty good. I'd gotten as far as houses.'

'Well, yeah, but people can live without houses. It's just less fun; where'd you put all your crap? And then you'd start asking, hell, why do I need all this crap? Questions, see, questions like that are dangerous. By and large we all get on better without them.'

'Holy crap. You're right.'

'Of course I am.'

'Maybe I've been asking the wrong question.'

'Alright. Hit me. What have you got?'

'Try this on for size. What can people live *without*?'

Another thoughtful drag. 'Television. Icecream. Student debt.'

Kate raised a finger. 'But *why* would you want to live without those things?'

Gary's kind eyes screwed up distastefully. 'Is this some cult thing? Are you joining a cult? Kate, honey, I can see you've been feeling down but I promise that surrendering your dignity so some charismatic asshat can drive a Bentley is not the answer.'

'Ha, nice. I already have a day job to fit that bill. And I haven't been feeling down, why would you say that?'

'Really.'

'I haven't been …' Kate blinked and found her glass empty. Now *that* wasn't right. 'I just haven't been feeling. There's no law against it.'

'Huh. Well you've dialled the right number after all. Let's sit you back on the clock.'

'Smooth. With seduction like that I'm frankly shocked you could squeeze me in.'

'Oh it's a tight schedule.' Then, 'Fucking hell! When was the last time you changed your sheets?'

'Leave it. I'll throw a towel over the couch.'

'Ro-mantic!'

Ever the gentleman Gary supplied his own rubbers, which was covered in the bill. After, he would even tie them with that efficient masculine flourish and could be relied on to take them away. A discretionary touch that implied either fear of voodoo or that not all his clients were single.

As always, Kate deployed a series of prompts not to lie there like a log. Not that she failed to enjoy it: *she* had called *him*. But the procedure seemed to be something her body craved, or ego, freeing her mind to dart about nibbling at its own worries.

Kate leaped bolt upright on the couch, hair mussed, the towel scratchy beneath her backside. Gary slid off and knocked the coffee table over with a crash. 'Ow! What the fuck!'

'I'm an idiot. Phoning about, chasing this elusive town. I can just drive there.'

CHAPTER THREE

ROADTRIP

Travel set a troubling precedent. It could hardly bode well for ongoing employment to draw attention to how much better the office ran in Kate's absence. And remaining was less inconvenient than casting about for some other job to despise just as vaguely. All merely to sustain this existence, which she also did not want.

Predictability being his middle name Supervisor Gary showed the whites of his eyes at the very idea of assigning her equipment or a vehicle. He'd made it very clear with a stabbing finger on his desk that not even a paperclip would be signed off this side of hell without witnesses to attest Kate had done better this time than holing up to drink herself into the emergency room.

Yet another landmine that drunk Kate had so thoughtfully peppered throughout her life. If that sot was never going to make anything of herself, she'd be damned if she allowed sober Kate the privilege.

So Lin tagged along, because bright optimists love car rides. Out of everyone in the office Lin alone could stand extended periods of Kate. Kate did not mind so much. Her family had kept a brace of retrievers, she was used to their slobbery perky ways.

Only one vehicle was available at the garage, the Orphan Annie nobody had wanted. You bet the two women were expected to say "thankyou" as well and mean it, which Lin did because she was a great big rube. Orphan Annie was less grey import than ghost. The itty bitty four wheel drive shuddered all over like it was terrified to be driven up the ramp into the sweltering day. Significantly worse as it got up to speed.

It also turned out to be imperfectly sealed enough to shelter an entire ecology. Cool air was but a rumour so as first order of business Kate slammed the vents shut, leery of eight legs slinking out while they were barrelling down the highway. Even as a child she had been obsessed by crashes, spent her entire time in cars holding her breath. They would be venturing so far out on this wild goose chase that nobody would stumble across the accident for days. Two twists of jerky by then, snarled into rusted metal.

Contemplating the trip Kate had feared the wider world would be an assault. Walls helped hold in the seep, after all, kept her safe in its numbing midst. So much so that condensation streaked the ceiling and her fingertips were always wrinkled.

To the very weird contrary the further their rattletrap lurched from the city the lighter Kate felt. As though simple sunlight was sluicing through and rinsing her clean.

There are things I could do without, she realised incredulously. She had always assumed her house to be tidily in order. And that begged the question, *would life be better without them?*

Lin was tuned in to the liberation as well. Possibly in a less dysfunctional way. She was charming to observe, rolling down the archaic hand crank to stick her forehead into the airstream with a deep *aah*. 'Oh doesn't that feel good! I love being on the move. Sometimes I feel like one of those train people, you know?'

'Hobos?'

Lin threw back her head and laughed. Strong profile in the sun, hatchet nose leading the way. Kate felt buffeted by her cheer and gripped the wheel tighter to keep them on the road. It was worth staying alert: the wildlife out here were bastards for flinging themselves beneath the tyres.

'Hobo, you're funny. Surely you've heard of this before. Sometimes when there's some big accident, like a train wreck, you get one or two people unaccounted for. Not mixed up in the casualties or survivors. Just … gone.'

'Did they vanish?'

'Not literally as in vaporised or anything.' Well no, Lin's tone drawled. That would be stupid. 'It's more like, um. Imagine they were going about their day which in this case I suppose involves trains. Same as any other day. And then suddenly bang! They just get handed this unexpected thing. This golden opportunity to walk out of their lives. So they take off.'

'What, just like that?' It hardly sounded like work-until-you-drop-in-the-traces human behaviour as Kate had observed it. Maybe she wasn't spending enough time on public transport.

Lin snapped her fingers. 'Just like that. No planning, no forethought. Real spur of the moment reflex stuff. These train people shaken awake by the crash, they look around with clear eyes and realise, *This life isn't right. This isn't what I expected.*'

Focussed on the road Kate allowed herself a noncommittal, 'Mm,' but Lin wasn't done.

'You see, Ms K, I reckon once things go off the rails everyone can be divided into two camps. To the left you get those who walk, the anomalous few. And to the right the majority, those who sit themselves down numbly in the ruins.' Even if they ache to go, staring after the escapees with exhausted eyes, they're too conditioned. 'Instead they quietly wait to be slotted back into their lives so's they can stare at a screen, read emails and pretend they never saw a choice.'

'That's … brutally judgmental. Really.' Would not have expected it of happy go Lin, although it shed uncomfortable light on the wellspring of her liveliness. 'Go on, then. Which are you?'

Kate was setting a trap. People with grandiose scenarios invariably leave themselves a back door, because of course such sweeping judgment could not possibly apply to *them*.

'Me? I'd be busy first aiding the shit out of people.'

'Aha! Everyone's the Superman of their story.'

As a matter of fact for the training credit Kate had dragged herself through the very same "Don't Panic!" first responder program, although she could not imagine anything worse than having to put it into action.

Ravelling bandages, counting compressions or trying to sort stroke from overdose did not spook her. No, the worst would be *imposing* herself. Intruding into lives when they were split and vulnerable. Kate strongly suspected herself likely to step back come the critical push, let nature take its course.

Depending on Orphan Annie's orientation they had to keep circulating their exposed arms into dapples of shade. Kate wore gloves to protect her hands on the wheel. The sun burned, licking determinedly with a scalding tongue. No slathering of sunscreen was enough, leaving greasy smears everywhere. Running with perspiration.

They faced a tricky job getting the upholstery clean enough for hand back, but Kate could not bear dwelling on their return. To feel the shackles of routine rattle back into place—no, not yet. Let the two plunge onward a while longer, exhilarating in the pantomime that there was true liberation to be had.

They stopped and peeled themselves from sweat soaked seats for late lunch at a pub. A rill of shops up main street, which was the through road and entirety of the postcode. These mini settlements clinging to the transit route were all there was to find out here and the further you ventured, the bigger the fuel tank needed to make it between such islands.

The air conditioned pub was wonderful to walk into. Glowing hardwood panelling and other details, including a host of carven angels, hinted the building's origin as a decommissioned church. Perhaps the oldest colonial structure out here, thrown up by settlers wanting to make this lonely place feel safe. Deconsecrating had not spoiled its lovely resinous hush.

Under stained glass with beery carpet as accompaniment, lunch was spectacular and generous enough to give them both food babies. The spread had to be extraordinary, to lure locals from isolated farmsteads.

It was the owner who brought their plates on veiny forearms, and who otherwise posted vigil behind the bar. Picturesque as the place was, who could afford staff these days? He did it because he loved the pub and continued even when he did not, for what other choice was there.

Kate twisted her glass to set charred looking sediment a-swirl. Her darker half would not let her leave the dregs so she strained them through her teeth, ignoring the bloodied aspect it lent. Pushing her plate aside she spread a roadmap on the bar, wet spots sinking through.

Kitchen benches not being terribly portable she had re-sketched the town on the reverse of this cheap map but that side remained down for now. She was not prepared to go flashing that around, even Lin had yet to see it.

'Excuse me. You know if there's anything out this way?'

The pub owner's eyebrows made for the cover of his hairline. Trees, the map said. Could she not read for herself? Out of date now following the burn but sure to come back at its own pace, plants then animals, if not quite the same. That was how the bush worked. If humanity blew away like smoke tomorrow it would set to taking back the country in the same manner.

The owner's amusement came tempered with tolerance. Drunks propped up his livelihood and he saluted the signs of that other Kate fizzing beneath her skin. Drunks could hardly be expected to act normal.

'Nothing, Miss, so far as I know. Nothing's out there.' But plenty in here, plenty of grapes, plenty of rye, the lips of the register sucking at their wallets.

Kate hardly expected better. 'There ever been anything you know of?'

He shrugged with teatowel riding one shoulder, a local gesture that meant a bit yes and a bit no. Then he turned and called down the bar. 'Hey, Dad!'

Advanced enough that it was ludicrous to imagine his progenitor still alive. They would have to be fossils. But incredibly one of the cigar stinking codgers who had been craning in a dark corner to watch television sighed, extricated himself and grudgingly waddled over. All wattled and seamed, the blue eyes filmy and adrift.

Left to her own devices Kate never would have disturbed the insular huddle. It was a stretch to sounding out the owner, and he had already broken the ice taking her order.

'Dad, these ladies want to know was there ever anything here. No, *here*, look, on the map.'

Refusing to be rushed now that everyone was paying attention the old lad tweezed specs from his plaid pocket. The lenses were thick enough to have serviced Hubble. He made a right song and dance of inspecting the paperwork, gumming his false teeth with a sound like mucus sucked through a hose. All three listeners including his son shuddered violently.

'Used ta be paddocks nearby. Not here …' he shifted Kate's pointing finger slightly, his lumpy touch like winter sticks on her skin. 'Here. But the farm went and got some sickness in the crop, couldn't make a go of it. Nothing since.'

A pause to see if there would be any more, and then his son topped up Old Dad's pint with dark flowing beer. Good boy for dancing for the tourists. Old Dad grunted. He had raised the little upstart; reap what you sow.

Lin nervously asked, 'What kind of sickness, exactly?' Her wattage of enthusiasm had dimmed markedly.

Old Dad made that awful sound in response: snail flesh clogging a drain pipe. It might have been a chuckle. The decrepit old sod might as well have been drowning in his lungs here in this baked town, thousands of kilometres from any shore.

'Purple lumps like contusions in the grain. Some kind a fungus. Can't recall the name. Swellings. Looked nasty, it did. Paddocks was for stock feed but good fuckin' luck offloading the stuff, couldn't afford the fancy machines to clean it. Chickens an' pigs staggering about, losing they eyes.'

'But couldn't they get rid of it? Spray it or something?' Lin's knowledge of agriculture was patchy at best.

'Tried deep tilling. Rotating crop for a couple of season. Couldn't entirely shake it no matter what, like a curse clung to their family. Eventually for the good of their kid if nothin' else they spat on the dirt an' let the bush have it back. Good riddance.'

Kate tried weighing him with her eyes but truthfulness, in any of its guises, was not her speciality. Willing to bet her foot if Old Dad hadn't a clue, something equally colourful would have spilled forth. She folded her map fussily; delicate with the waterlogged bits, it had to last out the day.

At that signal of conclusion Old Dad gave them the final up and down without much interest before stowing his glasses. What were two middle aged birds to him? Were they young and lush he might have at least embarrassed his son by leering.

The owner seemed to think dismissiveness was just as bad, which might be true if either woman cared enough to feel offended. 'Are you ladies expecting to find something out there?'

Kate smiled stiffly. At least, without checking with her hands she was reasonably sure that she did. 'Thank you for your help.' She would have loved to stay for a drink, would eagerly trade a kidney for the rest of that bottle but there was no avoiding the conversation that had been broached.

'And for the meal,' Lin echoed, dutifully sliding off her stool. 'It was lovely.' True, but Lin had chimed that exact same phrase everywhere they ate, even when they pulled over for indifferent petrol station coffee. It was some kind of social reflex.

They both sure felt it when they stepped outside the pub's roaring air conditioning. The renewed heat was a shove to the sternum. The temperature must have made the pub a popular refuge during the worst of the recent bushfire—far flung neighbours crowding in to usurp the old buggers' corner and monitor the blaze on the news. Step outside for a smoke and they could eyeball it for themselves: huge black oily sheets and pillars that rippled on the horizon. Never quite distant enough. It must have felt like an oncoming apocalypse.

Decide Early to Stay or Go used to be the official advice, the authorities quite rightly not wanting folk stranded trying to get out in a last minute panic. That was where victims used to perish: roasted in their vehicles at the end of a hideous succession of decisions.

Those were *Duck and Cover* days, before everyone came to grips with how a firestorm was a non survivable event. Inside your house or out, the very air burned. *Go* they said now *just go*. Legally problematic advice regarding property but you couldn't start over if you were dead.

'You know,' Lin ventured as they fitted sore buttocks back into Orphan Annie's seats for another round of rattling. 'A fanatic goes nowhere without her enabler.'

'Do you honestly believe everything comes in opposing pairs?'

'Just like Noah's Ark. Didn't you go to school?'

'Not crazy school.'

'Just saying, Ms K, that someday my turn's gonna roll around and I'll want to see a few favours back from you. Not one hundred percent crazy on taking a stroll through your little plague zone here.'

'Fungus. It's a fungus zone.' Kate briefly flirted with adding *Just don't eat the grass and you'll be fine*, but from there the tangle of inferred insult stretched beyond the horizon, they would still be arguing come midnight. Health was a big ticket concern for Lin. This week something to do with juices was in line to save the day, so she could understand the woman's discomfort with anything that impugned the food chain.

Clouds of dust fussed behind Orphan Annie from the dry fissured earth, even on tarmac. It would be worse when they ran out of sealed road. They knew they were drawing close when they found leaves baked right out of the trees, falling in flat sheets across the road. For a while the crackle beneath the tyres was their only conversation.

The hard barky smell of the trees gushed in the open window. Termite mounds flashed by, huge cones with red crumbs tumbling down their flanks, swallowing up gargantuan downed carcasses. Charging along only afforded tiny sips of the landscape they traversed. Kate and Lin were tourists.

'Here! Here, turn off here.'

As predicted, asphalt devolved into dirt track. Kate slowed abruptly enough to throw them both against the seatbelts. Progress would now be a case of picking their way between enterprising shrubs and smashed quartz fangs that would happily rip the undercarriage off poor old Orphan Annie.

It was a bit unnerving to no longer spy powerlines strung alongside, when you've been raised to take that kind of security for granted. Big tree limbs had come down and nobody had bothered to move them; one hooked beneath, to be dragged squalling for a few meters before it popped free. This was no place people ventured.

Which made it all the stranger when they came to a gate.

No fence. Only the gate, square and lonely across the road as though a house or more likely a manor had stood way out here once upon a time. Kate bit down a surge of vindication because the structure looked old. Extremely old.

The gate was bare, plain and brutal. Hardware that could have been picked up second hand from some mothballed prison for a song. Or a scream. That welded pattern—you could not help imagining emaciated faces behind it, pleading.

The posts to either side had once been decoratively sheathed by two cairns of dusty white stone, now partly tumbled into loose piles around the base. They resembled two lumpy old men with their pants down, which ought to have been humorous. If not for the diseased rust that bled out of gaps in the pale rock. It had trickled gradually down, drying in seasons, finally clotting the dirt they stood on. In contrast to the riotous bush on all sides nothing grew there. Nothing.

As she studied them Kate's gaze wanted desperately to veer away, go someplace else, as though merely the act of looking might draw their vile attention on you. The whole assemblage was so out of place it was like installation art. A sculpture of awfulness.

They idled before it until Lin shook her head. 'What are you staring at me for? You've already got gloves on.'

'Why not you? You're the passenger, the passenger always opens the gate.'

'Because it looks like two nasty old fellas having a shit in the woods, that's why not me!'

They could not sit here all day until they melted. Somebody had to be the grownup. Kate blew air out her cheeks and yanked the handbrake on, springs groaning. 'Your imagination's nasty.'

'Ms K, there's nothing wrong with my imagination.' Lin gestured through the windscreen. 'I'm not imagining that, it's right in front of us.'

Kate reluctantly slid out of the cab. The sounds of nature seemed very loud though in reality she was listening extra hard. Her senses trying to puzzle out which way to bolt.

'So, you put the handbrake on, right.'

'Yes mother. Wiped my backside after number two, too.'

'Good. Well … be careful.'

'Careful? Really? Thank heaven you mentioned, I was all set to lick the damned thing open.'

Lin gagged and snorted; but was quick to reach across and shut the driver's side door all the same. Keeping herself in safe.

As Kate cleared Annie's rattling nose and marched nearer her bravado faltered. Sure, it was hot. The haze nearer the gate seemed hotter somehow. Dizzying, like approaching an oven on full blast, the sweat baked out to make a salt crust.

Kate had not been allowed to play in the kitchen as a child, in fact her mother had shaken a real fear of hot appliances into her. That memory was a golden oldie; the stomach sickness so intense now that her teeth clattered. Quite the life lesson: it's not important to understand, only to be afraid.

The two piles of rock seemed to be staring back. Just daring her to defy good sense and inch closer. Even at this range they had a hot stink of human urine, horrid old piss, a Sunday morning miasma familiar to any urban resident. The stones were an oven baking trays of piss, sick rotten piss, cancer piss.

Kate grimaced and spat, and again without much saliva, trying to clear it from her mouth. She especially did not want to step up between them, which was of course required to reach the gate. Too vulnerable, she could not keep an eye on both even by whipping her gaze back and forth.

Kate reached out to put shaking hands on the gate …

BEEEP!

Kate almost shat her pants. Lin was cackling hysterically but the blaring car horn broke no tension, only an unbearable tightening that cramped and shivered. Lin's mouth gaping almost unnaturally behind the windscreen. Was that laughter? Her face looked curdy white.

For form's sake Kate spared time to flip her comrade a trembling double bird, only whirling around when she realised she had turned her back on both stone old men. They were so close, those sentinels. Had they moved?

Sly old piles of rock. They savoured the public airing of Kate's fear, saliva practically dripped out to see her weak. Brought low, little bunny. They knew what to do with little bunnies.

'COME OON!' Lin howled. *BEEEP!*

Only it was not funny, Kate detected the sobbing edge to her voice. Just get it done, Kate. Fast. Unpleasantries sometimes had to be managed, even if they made your skin crack and shrivel with the desire to be away.

Hating every second of it and holding her breath she unwound the strand of wire that held the gate closed. Gave it a push. Heat pouring off the two piles of rock crabbed to either side.

Impossible to think of them as deliberate constructs patted into place by sane hands. They must have accrued patiently into their current shapes over time; all the bad thoughts of the surrounding area coalesced into a stone that was hard and white and gleaming. Humanity had plenty of negativity to offer. The process squeezed rust-iron juice that bled from their hearts.

Scrambling back to Annie pressure burgeoned at Kate's back, a stormfront. She scrabbled helplessly at the handle, pounded on the window. 'Unlock the door!' Lin popped it and she slid back in, gasping, her heart set to break the one minute mile. 'You asshole!'

'I didn't lock you *out*. I was locking myself *in*.' Lin's play for redemption fell a bit flat.

'Asshole ruling still stands.' Kate gunned the engine and dropped the handbrake. For a heart stopping second they were roaring straight for one of the old men before she fishtailed and gained traction, sending them lunging past.

The sentinel did not flinch. Of course not. Kate must have imagined that.

'Aren't you going to shut the gate?' Only half serious.

'Fuck that gate. No, you. No, the gate.' She was going to toss these gloves, too, when she found a bin. Snuffled and shook her head; the old pee smell had somehow got inside. Might have to throw her lungs out, too.

They lurched along, bright panic fading and Kate wrestling the wheel for progress. Now they entered the burn's territory. The dark border seemed to rush at them across the landscape. It was immense, horizon to horizon, threatening to flip their shuddering vehicle as it flashed under the wheels. Here, finally, was the world as Lin had conceived it: cut perfectly in two. You would think she'd look happier instead of cringing down in her seat.

And then they were through, for better or worse. Normality receding behind them. Kate felt an irrational urge to lunge at her reflection, where surely lurked drunk Kate with her sparkling dark eyes, and scream *No I've changed my mind! Swap back!* To contain the compulsion she clamped her lips shut.

Here the ground was humped and black. Broken sticks poking through like spears missing their victims. A thick jumble of char. Heat stored in the matt charcoal was thrust sweltering back at the sky, energy entirely wasted. There was nothing left to absorb it, nothing to use it. All that seething living bush they had been driving through had been wiped away, nullified.

With tension pressing Kate's foot down they were still going too fast. The dirt of the path they followed was the palest thing about, peeping here and there through drifts of carbon. There had been nothing to burn on the rocks of the path.

The breeze was no longer refreshing and Lin wound up her window with a *that's that* briskness. Her brusque practicality, especially in a situation as wobbly as this, was wonderful. 'Fierce, wasn't it?' she observed, combing her hair back. 'Not surprising given conditions, it was so dry, with thick tangles of undergrowth. I'll bet that before the bushfire scraped it all off we'd never have fit down this track.'

Given the narrowness of Orphan Annie that was saying something. Kate was less blasé, genuinely dazed. It was one thing to study pictures from the comfort of your desk, quite another to be driving through a firestorm's aftermath. She had never been big on fieldwork.

'Everything's gone,' she stammered. 'The fire just bulldozed through as it liked and took down everything. Nobody bothered to stop it.'

'Are you kidding?' Lin scowled impatiently, not fond of the slowpoke holding everyone up. 'Council probably threw a party. Best opportunity to cull the deadfall in, what, fifty years?

A hundred? Should never have let it sit so long in the first place, let some other smaller fires have a gnaw at it.'

Lin looked mournful as another thought occurred. 'More animals would have escaped that way. There'd be more left.' Preventing burns altogether was disastrous the longer it went on, laying groundwork for exactly what had ripped through here: a firestorm.

'Might not have made any difference.' Kate rubbed her forehead, although the bouncing made her punch herself in the eye a bit. 'Once they get so big fires make their own weather, and then it doesn't matter what fuel's around. Would have been better not to ruin the climate so bad that fires get this mad in the first place. And it's not animals I'm worried about.'

'That's because you've got no heart. Or sense. Don't you think we're going a little fast?'

Kate turned her head, keen to let Lin in on her strict no back seat drivers policy. At the same time they lurched over the next rise and almost slammed into a fire department vehicle blocking the way.

By the time Lin mustered breath for a terrified squawk Kate was already skidding them to a jolting halt. Overstressed brake pads stank. Overstressed people probably stank too. Kate closed her eyes for a heartbeat, silently thanking fate that there'd been no bottle of wine at lunch. Clean reflexes for this very moment when it mattered.

She opened them again when Lin's shaky hand groped for her shoulder. 'Thanks for stopping.'

She would have loved to counter with something cool like, 'Don't mention it,' but her goldfish mouth fumbled. No matter. She fixed her eyes through the windscreen.

Two youths lounged on the white bonnet of the fire department's four wheel drive, its multitude of whip antennae beating an insectile tattoo above their heads. A guy and a girl, their strong healthy limbs close reflections of one another like an advertisement for puberty. When Orphan Annie had slammed to a halt at their very feet they hardly stirred, as though this was the most natural spot to haul up for a bit of sunbathing.

Foreshortened her view. All twenty of those languid exposed toes were painted the same trampy scarlet, a colour only the young or those trying to compete with them are drawn to. And the intense heatwaves shimmering off the hood distorted their faces into mouthless watery ripples beneath blank sunglasses. Flesh that dripped.

Kate did not need to be told there was a third in that car. The needling pain behind her eyes broke the news, a static rumble that was difficult to tune out and almost made it impossible to pretend to be normal. It was the far off threat of a firestorm sweeping in. Trees exploding, the very air igniting. It was a sound to make you huddle down in your bones praying for it to pass by.

She knew then who it was and her body shuddered violently, sharply and all over, trying to shake the revelation off. She pitied her poor skin for thinking that would work. No, she pitied herself. It was trapped animal thinking.

The fireman from the phone call surged cheerfully from the driver's seat to confront them. No glasses: unlike the fresh young horrors on the bonnet he had nothing to hide. His eyes stabbed back at her intently and Kate groaned at the rigmarole of a dick measuring contest.

It was not just the unnerving sound he emitted that made her leery. Violence was always on the table, the last argument, a masculine trait she had so often coveted. How much smoother might the thousand petty negotiations of life go with the unspoken understanding that one party could always *take* from the other. They were in the middle of nowhere. Who would know?

Lin was the one with the guts, the first to slide out and face the roadblock. She had not been recognised a woman at birth; not that you would know, plenty of girls were tall. In Lin's towering shadow Kate scratched together the courage to follow, throwing her gloves on the seat.

The firefighter approached with a cocky swagger. Fitting himself into the role of host, which made them interlopers at the mercy of his hospitality. Which party took control was often all in how you framed the opening exchange.

The body language Kate recognised with a sort of horror. He was *flirting*, and for a good looking lad like him it had probably taken him far in life. No further! The prospect profoundly nauseated—she just wanted to be left alone.

'Kate, I presume?' Hedging his bets as to who merited the radioisotope of his attention. Which best resembled a "Kate"? The first one, haughtily unfolding her length like a giraffe from a clown car? Or the little grey possum, stern face atop a body that found middle age as easy as slipping into a well fitting sock?

'I suspect you three are a bit late to the fire,' was Lin's tart opening salvo. The other two on the car, just as handsome as each other, grinned lazily but *Kate's* firefighter laughed right from the gut, making a jolly old point of it. He waved a broad gesture at the devastation around them. *Would you look at all this?*

Now Kate could see that he was one handed. His left arm ended halfway down the long straight bones of his forearm, in a knotted slickness that could only be an old burn. The same tissue also smothered his right hand, truncating two fingers but apparently leaving it functional. Once upon a time he had been left handed and had reached into something he should not have.

She wondered briefly how he managed their monster of a car, recalling how the wheel had fought her own hands, and then chided herself for asking inconsequential questions. He was clearly a good deal stronger. Always keep the last argument in mind.

'Billy,' he introduced himself, zeroing in on her at last. Lin's body language must have given it away, subtly deferential. Billy's handshake told of many hours of physical therapy, a man who would wring the best out of any resource he had. A man who did not quit.

The hissing fire static intensified briefly at his touch, she thought of Geiger counters rattling hysterically but was already getting better at screening the input out. 'This here's Sue and Sam. Got quite the tickle of curiosity following your call, so ...' That encompassing gesture again. Here we are.

Indeed. 'How did you know where we'd be?'

Now fireman Billy looked crestfallen. Must the credulous always clamour to see behind the curtain? Could there not just be magic in the world? For her part Kate flashed on suspicions of the pub, the too helpful owner or his ferrety gaggle of old men. Old Dad who had disinterestedly pawed her map.

But it was pointless to play pin the blame. If the man standing in front of her wanted information he was bound to sniff it out one way or another, infinitely creative. She had to remind herself to stand with shoulders back. Show no hint of oppression, give him nothing to latch onto.

'What do you mean, how did we find you? Kate, we're *firemen*. Firemen are awesome!' It would have been the height of obnoxiousness for the two on the bonnet to high-five each other; you could tell by the way their melting heads bobbed appreciatively they were considering it. Thankfully that sort of behaviour went out in the eighties.

Sam and Sue saw nothing sinister in the lengths their dear leader had gone to tracking down a stranger, all this middle of nowhere stuff was a lark. Nothing in them but laughter and goading. With such hounds at his back Billy ought to keep a sharp eye out.

At the sourness of Kate's face he relented, thrilled to tout his horn. 'Ok, so I've had tower lookouts keeping watch for you on the roads. Nobody else comes out this way. They radioed your car in, and we came to head you off at the pass.' Bright eyed like he was expecting mummy to pat his head.

'But *why*?' They weren't breaking any laws or hurting anybody. Kate was hard pressed to imagine how she'd goosed his ego to warrant such attention. The firemen had no business being out here with their slick grins sliding off their chins—the fire had gone out, right?

'I said. Curiosity. What more is there to a good life?'

Fortunately neither woman was the sort to whine about proceedings being unfair; they would hardly have accomplished so much if they were. Dismissed from the conversation and liking it just fine Lin was already hauling the day packs out of Orphan Annie. Busying herself with quick checks of water, compasses, sunscreen. It seemed excessive but they would be walking out of sight of the track, and this landscape had no landmarks for them.

Stories abounded of the unwary thinking they were just going for a stroll. Only last year a man lost in a national park had live posted his demise to the anguish of family and rescue services who had been utterly unable to pinpoint and save him. The news outlets had hotly denounced it as a hoax, rather insensitively as it turned out. But that was how badly society wanted to believe that in modern connected times vanishing was impossible.

At the time, hitting refresh for updates and sipping wine, the saga had reminded Kate of the lunar landing. The poor lost bastard might as well have been on the moon. Funding would have been shot if the world had to listen to those brave astronauts die out there in the dark, and there had allegedly been protocols to stop the broadcast in a fatal emergency. The disparity was in the audience. The similarity being how not being able to do anything was what killed hope.

'Kate!' Lin interrupted her thoughts, holding out a backpack. 'Let's go.'

'You won't find anything,' Billy insisted.

Kate refused to dignify him with a response but Lin smiled sweetly. 'If you're so sure, why don't you tag along?'

That lit his fire. At a curt gesture from Billy the pair sunning themselves slipped eagerly down from the hood to don shoes. Kate found it important to watch from the corner of her eye. Should she confront those faces head-on and find they really were running like egg custard, she would quietly drop off the edge of sanity. Easiest not to look. 'Lin!' she hissed.

'I know, I know. Creepy ass punks. But do you really want them hanging around our ride where we can't keep an eye on them?'

'... ok. Points to you.' Grudging points.

Wanting to be first from the path Kate fumbled the compass reading, as awkward as she'd ever been on school excursions. The key difference now being as an adult she'd learned small humiliations were survivable. Most of the big ones, too.

Once the sighting was taken on a burnt stick she could not look away, as all the burnt sticks were the same. The char shifted underfoot with dull crunching and squeaking and the heat, the heat. The heat was squeezing them: a marching row of stress toys about to get popped.

Although the furnace blast that passed for air failed to get any cooler, the day had decidedly turned. Sunlight came in sideways now, making the eyes water. Bloody across the landscape with little but sticks to arrest it. And those sticks cast long, sharp shadows, mockingly pointing the way. *Break your mother's back.* Everyone avoided standing on them;

nobody allowed themselves to admit it.

In the lead Kate clutched the compass like the Eucharist and stayed focussed on each target. She knew how cruelly kids with sore feet could malinger, adults would only be worse. She and Lin tried to ignore the aggressive *crunch crunch* trailing them.

The further they stumped the more Kate's heart sank. The seep correspondingly thickened, closing ranks around her. The layout of the town had been unmissable, surely they ought to have stumbled across it by now? She tried consulting the map in quick furtive glances. The two pups, being assholes who'd never fucked up, made a game of calling back and forth behind her rigid back.

'Find anything yet?'

'Charcoal! You?'

'No … wait … no wait yes … charcoal here too!'

She did not want to acknowledge Billy's sympathetic gaze on the back of her neck; the oppressive roar he emitted was more than enough.

Finally they came to a stop. The spindly shadows continued to point the way but they pointed nowhere. Drunk Kate was a fool.

Desultory, Lin kicked through some charred logs as though something might be hiding beneath. 'Ms K, I hate to admit it but there's nothing here.'

Kate heaved an angry sigh. 'Yeah.'

'Only that's *good*, right? People not getting burned to death is always a good thing. Maybe you did get it confused with that old institute somehow.'

Billy crunched up to join them. 'Wait, you don't mean the *Pillars* Institute? Man, I *wish* the fire had gone up that way. That place is asbestos central, you want to stay as far away from those old walls as you can get. Whole thing'll come down on some idiot's head someday.'

'Wonderful. Come on Kate, let's go back.'

The only bright point in a darkly exhausting day was how Kate's navigation brought them back to the road within sight of where the two cars sat facing nose to nose. Little Orphan Annie challenging Goliath.

'Kate.' Billy was offering something, his peanut gallery tittering behind him. 'Sorry you came all this way for nothing. Take this, I found it while we were kicking around out there. A souvenir.'

She turned the small pottery figurine over gingerly. About the quality your average kindergartener brings home, where the looseness of form becomes decidedly creepy. Eyes and mouth nothing more than three holes squashed into its face. It might have been a portrait of either of his two young friends.

Giving the smallest degree of nod that would pass as civil Kate slid into the car. She tossed the figurine into the passenger footwell with a shudder and Lin took it up for a look. Setting a new record she managed to hold her tongue until they were crackling their way back down the trail.

'Bull*shit* he picked this up while we were tramping about. I never saw him bend toward the ground. Look, it's not even dirty. And it rattles.' It did. A sound like a dry pea shaken in a cup. 'There's something inside.'

'Probably a listening device.'

'Or a homing device.'

'Or an asshole device. Definitely an asshole device.'

'Ha! It's gross enough. Looks like some kind of backwoods voodoo doll.'

That was a bit less funny. They juddered along in silence for a bit.

'Painkillers?'

'Centre console.'

'Ta. That squirt was so annoying, just being around him

was doing my head in.'

That was interesting. Lin could also detect the static the fireman was putting off. She just didn't know she was hearing it.

'So. Ms K. Billy-o sure didn't want us going anywhere near the institute, right?'

Kate slid her eyes sideways, the seep lifting a bit. 'You want to go check it out?'

'Absolutely. I bet it'll really roast his knickers.'

Chapter Four

Housewarming

'Ah, nope. Nope, Kate. I've changed my mind.' They rolled to a stop and shut off the headlights, letting gloom web them up. Lin was too loud in the confined space. 'This is rubbish. I don't like the dark. You don't like the dark. Hey—you know who fancies the dark, Kate?'

'Batman?'

'*Bad people*, that's who. It's where bad things happen and you can't see to save yourself *because it's dark!*'

'Lin,' Kate chided. She had to wait while a gust of wind rattled the car. 'Where's your pioneering fortitude?'

'I remember now, how could I forget: I left it up your mother's south pole.'

'How elegant.'

'Come ooon, Ms K.' There whined the golden retriever type, thumping its tail anxiously. 'Don't open that door. Don't, don't, don't … ah shit. This is the worst road trip ever.'

Kate tried not to feel stung by that, it was childish. 'We have torches. The bright portable light of civilisation … Uh oh.'

'What?'

'Oh no, Lin.'

'What!'

'Actually it seems I have the car keys and *both* the torches. Fancy that.'

Lin's eyes glittered. 'Say "torches" one more time. I dare you.'

'I am holding all the torches and heaven be my witness if you don't get your backside out of that car I will leave you here all alone. *In the dark.*'

'You wouldn't!' But the whole office was aware of Ms K's vindictive streak, the value of a good reputation. Lin petulantly slammed the door and held out her hand for a light. Gimmie, gimmie. Peering around fearfully.

The terrain that welcomed them was not quite full dark, but coming up fast. Just before the plunge, when the bloodied sky forces shadows face down into the dry choking earth and elongates them over kilometres. Anything familiar became lurid and strange. What a great time to be exploring an abandoned experimental complex.

In addition the wind had picked up, driving thick grey piled ahead of it. The concept of weather as a force to be reckoned with came grudgingly to the two urbanites. Nostrils shivered with the intimation of rain. Kate and Lin swept their lights about, tucking whipping hair behind their ears and wondering where to start.

Above, the treetops were heaving up in waves, tossing their heads like they wanted to bolt. Seasickness forced eyes down, to micro weeds poking through the gravel underfoot that nodded along to nausea.

In fact everything was overgrown, the bush ticking and scuffling on all sides. Competing flora clenched about the Pillars Institute like a sedge fist. And already the evening's first bloodsuckers swept humming into the torch beams.

Even back in its heyday the institute couldn't have been much to write home about. Little more had been done than backing in a trailer and scattering prefabricated portables around on the grass, trees pushed to the sides. *Close enough for government work*. At least this had been a human place. Its hauntings promised ordinary human memories.

Slab walkways connected the rickety structures, and a whole Eden of grass and wildflowers erupted from saggy gutters. A thousand straws spread across the back of the flat sheet roofs. The sight exuded such an aroma of underfunded public schools that it squashed both women down into feeling very small and vulnerable.

Kate had to fight a powerful déjà vu that their lives had somehow returned full circle, to find their discarded childhoods had been lying here in wait for them all this time. She had been a chubster, a sour-faced brat with a bowl haircut and a real trial to her parents. And Lin, well. Lin had much further to travel to escape the curds and whey femme in boy's clothing who'd been punched and spat on.

Adulthood slapped a veneer over the top but it never really went away. It was in humanity's nature to be horrid little bastards. 'You ever been here before?' Kate ventured.

'No. No way.'

'Looks familiar, doesn't it?'

'Nope,' Lin lied firmly, closing the topic. 'I've never been near a shithole like this in my life. So which shitty shit-shack do you want to tick off first? I reckon it'll be quickest to go anticlockwise, take the sinister way 'round.'

'Anticlockwise.'

'I'm all about efficiency. This paint look a little fresh to you?'

While inefficient Kate was mulling it over Lin suddenly flinched, and then leaped a few steps back as though a starter pistol had been fired. Banged her shin on the bumper and spooked Kate into jumping, too. 'Did you hear that? Tell me you heard it!'

'Not over the sound of you freaking out, no.'

Lin clicked off her torch and jammed it behind her back, as though that magically negated it ever having been lit. She was shivering in the humid air. 'I think there's somebody here.'

Of course. No matter how far you travelled there was the threat of people everywhere. However, as Kate ran a dubious eye across the site she spotted no trash. There was even trash on Everest. Here, the wind was really beginning to whip about but it blew no wrappers, not so much as a cigarette butt mixed in with the pebbles. Only the derelict structures collapsing quietly into the bush, and the smell of impending rain.

'I'm not sure, Lin. Let's have a quick look-see.'

Lin flatly refused to click her torch back on, claiming in a hiss, '*They* might see,' so Kate led the way. Many longing looks were cast back to the sanctuary of Orphan Annie, but having come so far Kate couldn't stomach the prospect of returning to her desk with nothing to show.

The first structure they dared approach was also the smallest, picking themselves an easy target. More along the lines of a tin sheep shed, really. As the hesitant women crunched their way nearer, the little pocket building that had seemed so innocuous reared up skittishly on timber stumps in silhouette against fading sky and oncoming storm.

It was enough to poke a nervous head through the doorway and ply the torch around the fusty organic litter. Quite enough. The structure did not even boast a floor, it had entirely rotted away. Torque your ankle slogging around in there. At odds with the dust-throated country without, it was a wet mulchy swamp to sink squalling into. Mosquito heaven.

Corroding tin walls, all sides. Just imagine the full hammering heat of noon with the midges singing. What livestock had huddled in here in fright of the worsening sky? Knee deep in the dank pit with eyes flashing white all around.

Beast stench stomped into the dirt. But were they not so very human, those primate teeth bared and wet? Familiar long limbs wound around? Piss leaking down skinny legs, burning sores along its path. The panic. The galloping panic of life slated a sole purpose and no acknowledgment of ambition, love or will beyond. No dignity for their existence.

Steaming hide rasped against the booming tin wall, leaving coarse tufts to linger long after misery, slaughter and table. To persist as memory, refusing to be sanitised.

Kate gasped as Lin yanked her away, and gulped down the thick air. She fancied a Saturday night steak as avidly as the next carnivore, but had almost converted right then and there.

Still at an adult march Lin towed her down the walkway to the next "classroom." They were not running, not yet, but her face was set in a *you and your stupid ideas* rictus. At least this was of a size to contain more than just the creeps. 'Open the door.'

'You open the door.'

'I'm trying … it's stuck.'

Metal squealed shockingly as the door came free, and they cringed together. The wind tore it clean out of bloodless fingers to slam gleefully against the wall, more noise, more racket, only now they were so stricken they scarcely noticed.

'What the hell?' Kate breathed, wide-eyed. *This* room had been tidied. A bit cobwebby and dusty, but still …

'Kate!' Lin worried at her sleeve, whimpering in fright. 'Don't go in. This is super-bad, ok?'

'But *look* at it!' A warp back to the time when mission brown roamed the earth. When the very fabric of space stank of tobacco. A shrine to some history they knew nothing about, that somebody had revered enough to do this.

Hesitant at first as they crossed the threshold, in case this was a past they might get trapped in and never be able to return to their own century. 'It's alright,' Kate murmured—nothing wrong with hoping.

As they poked tentatively about it became clear the mystery curator had not entirely kept the years away. The vinyl over the heavy steel chairs was cracked, extruding fistulas of disintegrating foam. Shelves of ring binders held papers as yellow as old teeth.

The desk that time forgot sat regally in the centre, gargantuan and unforgiving. Somebody had secured it at considerable trouble to counter the impermanence of the site—a statement of resolve: here I stay. Now that owner was long gone; whatever else the room might aspire to must always negotiate the encumbrance. It would have required a block and tackle to shift, little wonder it had been abandoned.

Kate had seen its like before—any moment her old headmaster might roost there like a crow in polyester pants. She shook her head sharply to rattle it out. She was a grown woman now. Grown women weren't browbeaten in the same way as a sensitive child; or should you try it, God help you.

From a stack on the imposing desk she gingerly flipped open a notebook, expecting the lot to collapse into spores and fust. A bolt struck into her head like grounded lightning. Voices. All different. All raw with desperation.

*… they'll be watching for us, oh yes must be ever so foxy now … never back, never, not on my life but onward, **through**, I'm determined … so very far. Hardly imagined it would be so far … this place … just isn't as I dreamed, I know, selfish to the*

end … if it kills me…

She let the pages whiffle shut, wishing she could erase the brief contact from her fingers. Quite possibly the skin would have to go as well.

Lin, blessedly normal Lin broke Kate's daze. 'Kate! Hey, Ms K! Shine your light over here.'

Kate's thundering headache pulled back a bit. 'You are holding a torch you know.'

'Oh. Right.' Up the back Lin had found a vast map of the region, the sort you expect to see unrolled in war rooms. They already had a suitable desk. All that was lacking were moustachioed generals gathered with their cognac, far from the slaughter and slog.

Kate joined her. The chart had been messily varnished right onto the back wall. Amber streaks and blobs ran down to harden at the base as though a living tree had been cut into. With sensitive fingertips they could trace long ago bristles. Neither elected to touch it for more than a curious moment. The surface looked sticky, a literal honey trap. Peculiar for it to be so cool and hard, denying entry.

'Maps,' Kate murmured. Boil landscape down to a scale you could comprehend and hang over it like a god. Spheres of influence were drawn on this map, rippling out across the terrain from an invisible stone dropped through the heart of things. An alarming crimson splash for the inner circle, shading out the further you went until reaching presumed safety.

Only two manmade locations were marked within that baleful red epicentre, neither quite at the middle. There was the institute, the very place they were poking around with their torches. And a farm. Kate bet she knew which farm that had been. She feared she was carrying a further ace up her sleeve. A third site.

When she held her stained, hand sketched map up against the wall they could both see what they had come looking for. Right in the eye.

'Is that what you saw?' Lin whispered, appalled. 'Oh shit, really?'

Kate was grinding her molars to dust. She snatched the map back down, stuffing it protectively away in her pocket. 'We stood there, Lin. There wasn't any town. It doesn't exist.'

'I'm beginning to buy that about as well as you do. Shush— yeah I *know* what we saw. I'm not daft. But look at the chart! Something's not right here. Sod it, I wish I'd brought my detective hat.'

'It's an actual hat, isn't it?' An enabler was exactly what Kate needed, her own efforts had left her exhausted. And a cog somewhere had engaged for Lin. She was into this now, in a big way.

'Let's check out the rest of the site. See if there's anything else.'

It had become proper grown up dark outside. The wind roared in fits, hurrying them along and gritting their sinuses with fistfuls of dirt flung through the air. It ought to feel safer not being able to see the tips of the trees convulsing above their heads, but the sensation of restless motion was dreadfully unsettling.

Lin started flicking her torch around like a strobe. In quick panicked bursts she succeeded in illuminating nothing, reminiscent of being catastrophically drunk. Kate was about to tell her to knock it off when the taller woman grabbed her arm and with a yank flattened them both against the side of the building. 'Ow! I need that arm for arming!'

'There's someone out there.'

A sick wave slapped against the sides of Kate's belly. But Lin had already selfishly cornered the market on panic and one of them had to keep a straight head if they were going to get out of this. 'Where?'

'Out past the buildings. In the trees.'

Kate took a deep breath, and pushed the urge to bolt for the car out with it. 'Ok. Ok. You stay here and flash your light around. Make some noise like we're talking.'

'I already don't feel good about this.'

'I'm going to sneak up behind them.'

'You *what*?'

'I've had enough, I'm sick of strangers watching what I'm up to! And there's two of us and only one of them.'

'You don't know that! There could be *hundreds* of them— in the dark, remember? Now is not the time to be drawing your arbitrary line in the sand!'

'Lin. Please be helpful.'

'Oh, I'll be helpful. Helpful when we're both dead.'

'At least I'm leaving you a torch.'

'Yay, remind me to thank your dead ass.'

It took more fortitude than Kate had to switch off her own light and plunge around the far corner, but she was already committed. Trailing the fingers of her free hand on the wall gathering splinters, chips of paint and spiderwebs. *Sneaky, sneaky*. Not a lot she could do about the gravel, which sounded like ice crust breaking. Nothing more than try and move with the fitful wind.

It lifted the heart in every lull to hear Lin nattering dutifully away. As animated as she ever was with a partner, which raised interesting points as to whether the second was required at all.

Kate had to stop before abandoning the building completely for the void, even though she could hear her colleague becoming progressively shriller. Held her breath, a nervous tick. Lin was warmth behind, but all was silhouettes and strange slithering up ahead. Things Kate strained to hear, then harder to forget.

There was only so much adapting her vision would do. Finally she made out the stiff upright figure her coworker had spotted. Her heart was stumbling. This might be a really bad idea. In outline, which was pretty much all she was getting, the watcher looked bulky and brutal. And so still. Staring toward Lin so intently.

It was unnatural. Like Lin was all that existed in the storming shaking world and he could not take his searing gaze off her for a second. Unwavering regard that would burn her and her happy chirping to ash where she stood.

This understandably pissed Kate off. She was disgusted and scared all at once. Such men yelled at women on the street, a daily indignity, barking like dogs and no telling which might chase you down the road. Accumulated sick boiling anger made her hands tremble to brain the mysterious figure with her torch from behind, spill every slick wormy thing from between his ears into the gravel and weeds.

Instead she ground her teeth harder, forcing herself down the civilised, tamed route. Kate flicked her torch on and bellowed, 'GOT YOU!' in a voice raw with rage and no small measure of peeing-your-pants terror. Dazzling light burst out.

Her torch beam pinned a cairn of old stones in place, moss spilling out of crevices like seeping cracks in its elephant hide. She had launched her sneak attack on a fucking pile of rocks. Her whole body clenched for confrontation, Kate struggled to reorient.

Had the cairn *shifted* with an awful jittering motion before the light locked it in place? Easy to dismiss as a trick of paranoia if not for that now familiar whiff of sick hospital waste. Surfaces never cleaned properly. Contamination.

Lin screamed.

A nerve stabbing peal Kate had never expected to hear outside of a horror movie. She had made a dreadful miscalculation.

'Lin! Lin, I'm coming!'

Kate charged back through the bushes so fast she might have folded space. Adrenaline wiped everything, a clean slate for running and a good way to get an eye poked out. Only later would she count the stinging wheals riddling her arms and face.

Pushing against the wind and its mocking *whoo* that staggered her, *ooh, you'll be too late Kate*, she came hammering around the corner wired to punt an attacker into the middle of next century.

Lin was haranguing a stranger at the considerable top of her lungs. '… you frightened the *life* out of me how *dare* you sneak up on people like that …'

The poor man held hands up in pleading defence in front of a dinner plate round face. Cheer was the natural setting for those features, so at the moment he managed to look cheerfully terrorised.

'Wasn't sneaking!' he protested, shielding his eyes as Kate put the torchlight threateningly on his face. Without a lot of experience for moments like these she was aping what she had seen in gangster films. 'Why would I be sneaking? I'm the caretaker!'

While Kate was nowhere near as pasty-wastie as Lin, she got why this fellow had seemed to pop out of nowhere. He was like a piece of enamelled night. Glints only off anxiously smiling teeth and the whites of his eyes. And he was dressed as drably as the landscape, a bit old fashioned as though somewhere he'd confused "caretaker" with "gameskeeper."

Lin was still at full steam. At her feet her broken torch lay where she had dropped it, and she clenched her long hair captive against the building gale—even that was done with tacit disapproval of the free way the stranger's untidy curls bounced about. '… what kind of *asshat* thinks scaring people is *funny* …'

Kate picked up the torch. 'Take a breather, Lin.'

'I'm sorry, miss. Sorry, right?' The tirade faltered but Lin's lips vibrated with indignation, clearly unpacified. He took a risk and extended the peace handshake. 'I'm Eric. I'm *supposed* to be here.'

While they were flapping awkwardly in the gale wondering how to progress, the first drops of rain came down hard as flung marbles. Eric who had been anticipating the onslaught ducked and grimaced, although it still looked friendly. He did not appear comfortable showing much range of emotion. 'You'd best come in. About to get pretty feral out here.'

Kate forbore to mention they had trespassed inside the office building already. If Eric failed to connect the door carelessly left to bang back and forth with his intruders, it was hardly her place to clarify.

Rain rattled across the roof, underscoring the dubious pleasure of being indoors. Eric meandered about the room clicking on lanterns, the blue-white variety that instead of giving a warming glow cut faces into cavernous shadows. But blue-white was great for conserving batteries, a key consideration outside the comforts of the grid.

Three creaking office chairs were pressed into service. Eric wiped them down and fussed them into a neat communist circle rather than caretaker versus intruders, all the while pretending not to notice the women studying him. They were wondering how to slot the meticulous host into the outdated room.

Their shelter fairly shuddered as the storm slapped it. The night seemed petulant at their refusal to run out and cavort in the dark amid shoddy buildings and prickly trees, stones that slithered and stacked themselves into leering piles. Eric settled himself. 'And you are ..?'

'I'm Kate, and this is Lin. She's not precious about sitting on your dusty chairs at all.'

Lin stuck her tongue out and finally planted her backside, completing the circle. Eric stroked his chin in the thoughtful manner of a man who had always wanted a goatee. 'Let me guess. Sightseers? That's all the Pillars Institute gets: spook hunting rubberneckers, or horny kids with spray cans at the ready.'

'Yep. That's us. Horny kids.' Lin made him laugh, it was her gift. Metal clanked against the chair as Eric chuckled, and her sharp eyes went straight to the military surplus canteen and several long handled tongs dangling from his belt. 'Who are you supposed to be, then Eric? Baron Barbeque?' Giving him an excuse to laugh again.

Kate sat back and watched. Lin thought it normal to be liked because the woman she had built herself into was attractive and genial. She flirted lavishly because it would get her things, sensitive only about her hands which she fussed to conceal in pockets or her long hair. No polish or rings, nothing to draw the eye. Kate found the neuroticism charming, fond of bright Lin.

'Barbeque ..? No, these are for picking up garbage. Lots of stuff you come across at the institute isn't nice to touch.'

Thinking of the notebook that had all but leaped up and bitten her, Kate was nodding before she could stop herself. The wind threw itself at the building again and this time the room actually boomed, making all three jump then snigger uneasily at themselves.

This was a tired, used up place in the searing blue-white light, dust burning off the lanterns. It had endured being scraped out and repurposed time and again until, scuffed and ringing with exhaustion, it ended up here. Kate was a lot more comfortable here than she ought to be. Briefly emboldened she took the lead. 'So, Eric. What are you doing?'

'Me? I said, I'm supposed to be around.'

'The caretaker, yeah, I get that. But you're *living* here.'

Lin looked shocked but it had been plenty obvious to Kate. He was too well set up to be merely visiting. Eric must have a solid reason, because from her brief poke around Kate had an idea this was nowhere nice folk should abide.

Eric wavered.

'I'll tell you ours if you tell us yours?' Lin temped. The room rattled again in warning, loose lips, ladies and gentleman. That made Eric glare at the ceiling with rebellious fire. Nobody told him what to do, not the weather or anybody. Born in another age he would have made a fabulous beatnik.

'Sounds fair. You two want a beer?'

Lin demurred, beer was hardly her thing. Kate practically launched herself at him and Eric's face took on an edge of caution, although not without compassion. After handing her a can and taking one himself he shut the lid of his esky firmly, sliding it back out of sight beneath the desk.

Here was a man who had already subsisted in that circle of hell among the self-medicators. He had borne witness to every slow second of their disintegrating lives, and would be no pal of hers in that regard. Well fuck him then.

Understanding reached, Eric resettled himself, tucking both hands primly in his lap. Too proper. It was most likely camouflage: contrary to the abashed grin beneath dark wary eyes Eric was certainly not as young as he seemed. The public would have proven predictably leery; as, to a lesser extent, they treated Kate for being a sullen mouthed woman and Lin for daring to be tall and bold. Life was all about where you fell on the sliding scale of bigotry. With no other victims, the very last human left clinging to the skin of the earth would still contrive to hate themself.

'You're right. I *am* living on site,' Eric fessed up. Lonely from being stranded, more than ready to talk. 'I'm looking for my brother.'

'Wait, there's *more* of you living out here?'

He made an odd noise, sarcastic and sad. 'Not living, no.'

Lin was instantly mortified, as she should be. 'I am so sorry.'

'We weren't close or anything. I've heard about him my entire childhood but we didn't even meet. Mum always called Ben her bad luck boy. Bad luck he got noticed. Bad luck his skin was just that bit lighter, you know?'

'Oh fucksticks,' Lin breathed. 'They took him, didn't they? That's what they did back then.' These atrocities that prick and squeeze national identity. In a country where the authorities could get away with *that*, well, there was no ground beneath your feet. Anything might be done to you.

'If by "back then" you mean they just gave it a nicer sounding name and kept on. Broke my folks. Broke both of 'em too bad to fix, so when I came along that was the parents I got. Sooner I could get out on my own the better.'

'You've got a brother you've never even met,' Lin marvelled.

'My folks almost didn't find out he'd been taken, even. At first Ben was visiting the district dentist, no big deal, come back in a few hours. Next thing my parents are being told to their faces oh your son died. *From a bad tooth?* Bad luck, they were told, can't beat it, go home now. They couldn't be shoved out of there fast enough. My folks weren't really human to the people at that clinic. Not proper people.'

Kate rubbed her goosefleshed arms. Thought uneasily of the confines of a claustrophobic shanty that *ought* to have been for livestock. Shoulders blundering against hers in the dark, knocking her askew, the torch wrenched from her hand …

'So my parents could hardly manage to walk out of there. Thought they were doing the right thing, bringing him in to get his teeth checked; can you imagine being told *Oh your kid's dead, fuck off now*. Mum was going to be sick. She put her hands over her mouth and they smelled like Ben's hair and she just started bawling. The whole world had fallen in.

'Some hygienist snuck out the back door, she caught up to Dad in the parking lot and pulled him aside. She'd seen Ben getting shoved in a ute. Nobody was supposed to talk about it.

'She didn't care for my folks either but getting told to her face what she could 'n couldn't talk about had hit her right in the spite. Actually spitting in my Dad's face with the force of getting it out, so pleased she was sallow with it. And he was a solid sort of fellow so he just stood there and took it, took down that dark poisonous knowledge like a long drink. Thank God for human nature, huh?

'My parents, one weeping blood and one stewing in venom, cleared out before security came to put the boot in but you can be sure they had no peace after that. I was on my way, preeclampsia kept Mum at home but Dad went out searching for Ben every day. He'd stalk utes like he hoped his missing son had been circling out there in a holding pattern for months, years, just waiting to be found. Almost got himself run over plenty from trying to peek in the windows, and it wasn't always by accident, either. Assholes on the way home from the pub.

'Missed my birth, of course. Missed out on the whole thing. Mum did alright by me but no secret it was only 'cause she had to, she wanted to be out looking as well. She'd often vague out and stare, stare hard like if she tried enough she could imagine herself to where Ben'd got taken. We did a lot of waiting, the two of us.' Empty rooms were all Eric could conjure when he thought of his childhood. Grey light falling in empty rooms.

'Dinner congealed by the time Dad came home with tyre prints on his shirt. Until Dad stopped coming through that door. That was it for me, I'd had enough. Sold everything not nailed down and busted my ass to get out to school, then TAFE among people who weren't fucking crazy, pardon my French. People who'd sit down and have a decent conversation with you, and help find support, scholarships, donations. Hardest thing I've ever managed. Did things I'm not proud of.' If it sounded trite that's how he was telling it. The doors were all closed.

'Mum passed, but with me out of her hair she at least got to spend her final years doing what she'd always wanted. Once both Dad and Mum were gone it was like Ben and his bad luck had vanished right out of reality. They were the only ones who cared about him.

'Me, I never thought of him at all until I finished studies and ran up against "What now?" I'd cut ties with everything to go to school, my history, lost it all. Only ever studied because it got me out of home. So nowhere to go and literally nothing to do when I got there. On top of a student debt that could buy Greece.

'None of which makes an attractive prospect. My girlfriend buzzed off just as I was nerving myself to propose. Know it sounds childish but it was the shock of her being gone that got me thinking seriously about death. The death of things: here I'd built up this future in my head and now it died. And that got me onto wondering about Ben. Like, so long as somebody had cared about him he still existed. And maybe my folks were so obsessed because it was their way of keeping him alive.

'That was when I missed Mum and Dad for the first time. Guess my family's always been about being too late for things. Soon my lost brother was all I could think about; all that seemed worthwhile, anyhow. I had some of their notes and hints that I'd always meant to throw out.' That was an understatement. Eric had inherited a whole suitcase of crazy as his sad maternal estate. 'Started my first scrapbook. Eventually led me here.'

These two nice looking ladies maybe did not need to hear how he had gone back and tried to burn down the dental clinic in the middle of the night. With modern fire codes it had never caught. His grand gesture just a charred dumpster out back.

'Your brother was at Pillars Institute? They dumped kids here?'

'All sorts got brought out here. Their astoundingly bad luck. So here I stand—sit, rather. After all these years I've turned out just like my folks. Difference is, someday I'm going to be able to visit Mum's grave and tell her where Ben is.'

'And what will you do after that?'

For an instant before he collected himself the look Eric flashed them was no longer haunted, but terrified. There was no "next." His life's centre was this one thing, and all beyond was blank. 'Guess I'll jump off that when I come to it.'

At least he had managed to answer Kate's question: why would anybody exist off the grid, why scratch after indignities modern convenience had already solved? Because it was the only way to get where you were headed. Only Eric had not gone anywhere. Brooding in isolation, putting the ducks of his past in a row. Confession building until it had to spill to the first idiots who'd listen.

'And what about yourselves?'

This might be Kate's dog and pony but poor Lin was stuck fielding questions. Fine. If Kate wanted to sit and frown silently like a hag let her. 'Well … you know that big bushfire went on near here recently?'

Eric's nod bounced his curly fringe about. 'Do I! Heart was in my mouth the whole time watching that black sky. Was gonna have to evacuate on foot if it turned this way, maybe follow the creek out.'

Easy to see from his twisting fingers that scenario would have had no happy ending. Imagine stumbling blind through the smoke with your lungs practically dragging behind you. Slapping at embers raining down, keep moving, if they set fires ahead you'll be done for. Body closing up shop beneath the furnace strain. The lack of air. Curtains falling one by one.

Lin pressed on. 'Ms K here was in charge of reviewing some info about the land afterward. It wasn't even supposed to be important, just routine check the box ... well.' She trailed off in puzzlement.

Eric lurched to his feet, it looked as though an invisible fist had seized and jerked his strings. His heavy chair rattled backward. He was staring, aghast, at Kate, only at Kate. Afraid he might drop to his knees or pitch a fit or something she stood, too. Lin got up so as not to be left out.

'Oh holy shit,' Eric breathed. 'You've seen the town haven't you?'

CHAPTER FIVE

BREAKING GROUND

By rights the atmosphere next morning ought to have been frosty. Eric—the aggrieved party, as he was now known—was off mustering clothes while the car cooled. Lin had offered a lift to main street, with a dark glare at Kate, it was really the least they could do. Luckily the prospect of a run at the laundromat was too good for nursing grudges.

If anything tender hearted Eric seemed sorry for Kate. Discovering she could still feel the worn reflex of shame made matters worse; which might have been his plan, but sounded more like her own nasty imagination inhabiting her sullenly pounding head.

Besides, "frosty" was a joke. Caught up in playing detective yesterday they'd not shown the brains to park in the shade;

now, the storm having sulked off overnight, Kate and Lin stood about with the car doors open waiting for the furnace inside to roar away.

Kate coughed. Swabbed sticky lips and eyes with the back of a palsied hand. Come steamy dawn her awareness had clicked on, sharp and unforgiving, like a switch. Access to last night's void remained limited—the toppled cooler and beer cans strewn about told the tale.

Seductive, that non-memory. She poked it like an ulcer and was rewarded with flashes nasty enough to effect hasty retreat. Lin was not buying her claim to amnesia. Judgmental was a posture speciality of Lin's, she leaned on Orphan Annie with crossed arms, giving it all she had. 'You're a different person when you drink, you know.'

'Mm.'

'I think it's more obvious you don't care about people.'

Damnit, why did the noncommittal *mm* never work? 'Hey, I care.' Although at that precise moment not so much. 'It's easier to do in the abstract.'

Lin shook her head sceptically, hair swinging. Like she knew more than she was letting on. Folk were always doing that—they hinted maddeningly at some profound insight from which sober Kate was barred. Ah, fuck 'em.

Conversation wilted as Eric appeared, thank God. Kate got banished to the back seat. No way was she good to drive, and the front was for righteous grownups. The laundry bag got parked next to her, exuding a furry eau de mushroom that had her hanging out the window.

Bright and bushy tailed Eric chatted amicably to the side of Lin's head and she winced and swore and bumped them down the track to the road. Not the most confident driver, and another red card against Kate's disgraceful ass for making her do it.

For her part Kate was concentrating so fiercely on keeping her stomach wedged in that she caught zilch of their gossip. Her skull vibrated against the frame. Could hardly hurt more than it already did.

She didn't perk up until coming into main street when they encountered a familiar white monster of a four wheel drive, its flanks streaked with crimson dust. Felt very much like being a rabbit passing some carnivore in the long grass, and if not already in a bath of sweat she would have broken out. The rabbit sneaks, counts desperately on not being worth a snap, except in cruel fun.

It seemed their return to the neighbourhood was unexpected: eyes goggled both ways across the strait. Kate felt obscurely better having Eric with them, although no telling what help he'd actually be in a crisis. Three on three, the odds were better balanced.

Lin smirked and flipped the firemen a friendly little wave. 'Never too early for asshats, huh?' Hopefully lipreading was beyond their remit.

Paranoia twisted Kate in her seat to follow the lumbering behemoth. She was the only witness to its wobble of indecision before swinging a wide u-turn in their wake.

Anxiety, or acid bubbled up her throat. Too sick for this shit. She put eyes resolutely forward in case she'd inadvertently invited them just by looking.

When they swung over to let Eric out nobody could miss the way the four wheel drive cruised slowly past, shark-like. Then it darted around a corner with tyres squealing and was gone.

'Hope those idiots don't dick around like that on streets with kids about,' Lin muttered balefully. Fat lot of good she could do except read about it in the paper if they did.

Having disembarked the good ship Orphan Annie Eric clutched his laundry and shuffled foot to foot. Kate clocked that dance from her glory days: he was hoping for a phone number. Reluctant to watch any connection to his fabled town go toodling off into the sunset. 'You two heading back to the ant hill?'

Soft handling to allow them a gracious exit, see ya later bum, but Lin responded with uncharacteristic firmness. 'We're not done here.'

This was fascinating. Kate craned across the seats, swallowing nausea as she subjected her head to the jostling. 'We're not?'

'Ha! Not even, sunshine. Today I'm all over researching the poisoned farm of doom.' Which was classic Lin. Anything rattled her, especially on the health front and she was prone to biting in. With knowledge she took back power. 'I'll need the car for a bit.'

'But …' Kate waved her hands weakly, unsure where to gain traction.

'*Think*, Ms K. We've got the gross farm and, a tad further out, Eric's weird institute; the two closest spots to that town of yours, in fact the only manmade things in llama distance.'

'Llama distance?'

'You know, spitting distance. And they're both ruined.'

'Lin, *everything* out here's ruined. The economy tanked.'

'Let me put it to you another way.'

'That's what *he* said.'

'Stop it, you're not funny.' A smirk crept round the edges regardless. Serious Lin was never fated to last. She leaned in to whisper. 'These two rather unsavoury locations are all we have. Unless you're ready to go home?' Her dark intent eyes but a whisper away, well intruding on Kate's comfort zone but she was too astounded to even put a hand over her death breath. In fact Kate practically gasped a noisome cloud into Lin's face.

She was absolutely right! They'd no reason to go dragging home and every excuse to push on. Hell, technically this was a job, they were getting *paid*.

If not for the seats and general lack of hugging acumen Kate would have embraced her. As it was she sat back. 'Right. Holy hell, you're right. Guess that leaves me the institute.' A flash of irritation that the tall woman had bogarted the most promising site, but the farm was the one Lin found upsetting so of course she would insist.

During the debate Eric's curly top had been whipping back and forth like a tennis spectator. Now he burst out in a smile like the sun coming up. Even knowing the truth it made him look awfully fresh and young. 'There's a motel down the way you can check into?' he volunteered, too tactful to note Kate's state outright. 'And it's not so far back to the institute without a car. I usually take the school bus and then hike up from the road.'

Kate would have scowled if she were not already so wretched. 'Thanks.' And at a growl from Lin, 'And I'll be sure to replace your beers.'

'Nah, no need. Got 'em when I thought I'd be bored, as a sort of experiment but, you know, the institute's hardly a fun spot to get so …' he slid her a cautious look, '… off your guard, yeah?' There was that aggravating expression again. All the world privy to something profound, a game-changer. Whatever. She could not waste her life wondering what drunk Kate'd been up to, it was bound to be along to bite her soon enough.

'Well go on Ms K.' Lin might have been ushering a reluctant preschooler—oh, she'd get hers soon enough. 'Off you pop. Have a good time.' Flipped the front seat forward to let her out.

Oddly reluctant to abandon the protective metal shell, Kate prodded her dishrag body across the seat and onto the baked pavement beside Eric. They looked like two scolded children ejected from the car, not daring to look at one another. She wished she could muster enough vinegar to slam the door without her head splitting open.

'Oh,' Lin added out the window with malicious good cheer. 'Be sure to give the boss a tingle, let him know how we're squandering his hard earned budget.' Knowing full well Gary wouldn't believe a word that came out of Kate. Orphan Annie shook with her laughter as she pulled away.

The motel being nominally en route Eric walked Kate there, and offered a sympathetic pat at her shoulder before moving on. 'Guess I'll catch up with you later.'

'Sure.' Small wonder he stuck to his guns and camped, if this was the accommodation to be had. A long spindle of unattractive brown brick, with identical beige rooms running down both sides. A transitory structure hearkening from the same "slap it together" era as the institute, to be squatted in by souls on their way to somewhere better.

Make that farting, perspiring, down-at-the-heels souls. People had sighed their exhaustion into the upholstery a hundredfold, left behind when the rest had been scraped and hosed away. A bodily continuance that defied erasure. Anyone else would have felt draining defeat to be slumped there surveying it.

Kate actually relaxed a little. Here finally was a place you could fade softly into the background. Each detail of the room a source of sardonic delight. Slivers of soap in crinkly packets that would never foam no matter how you rubbed, probably rendered from donkey fat in third world countries. An upturned water glass left a ring on its vintage paper doily.

The ugliness was comfort, it promised to whistle home the seep. And surely that clammy blanket would dispel last night. There was no dignity to what she recalled: stumbling in the dark, shoved this way and that by the vindictive wind. All the while unable to find the idiot threat of a loose tin door that arrhythmically hammered, hammered out there.

Lose her precious groping fingers, she would when that rusty edge slammed home. Then where would she be? Pulled down by pain, whimpering, into the muck. Unable to see, assess the damage. The keening wind. If she did not keep those wriggly fingers to herself …

The jolt of waking up was like startling into her own skin. Poised on the threshold of the motel room, the sun behind and dim coolness on her hands and face.

Well go inside, idiot! The last thing Kate needed were rumours about the weirdo at the motel, out here they'd be on any bone you threw.

She longed to hide in peace for a bit. Go underground. It was tricky to decide what she was dying for: a shower or a nap. If only there could be some glorious blend of the two which did not include drowning.

Perhaps she'd even rub one out if she could muster the enthusiasm, did wonders for her state of mind. But first she had to call Gary. And not fun Gary. Like all chores in life necessity before sweet, it was how grownups punished themselves. Just pray you still had enough energy to make it to the sweet someday.

'Katie-o!' Supervisor Gary always commenced on such an almighty high. Thought he could stave off the inevitable plunge. 'How are you two getting on? On your way safely back, I hope.'

Smug, thy throne be Kate's. 'Actually we found something.'

Gary's pause was too long to be strictly polite. 'Really?' he ventured. Of all the employees under his wing, Kate had a particular knack for ruin.

In the background a silvery voiced kettle began to sing, sing straight through Kate's sinuses. Even the clang as it came off the range was beautiful, like an antique bell brimming with water. Her mouth was instantly so cottony she wanted to blast her way down the phone and rip the cup of tea from his fingers.

Of course Kate knew she was not craving tea—her age was difficult to achieve without succumbing to bouts of self awareness. What she longed for with tooth shattering intensity was that showroom existence. Where somebody tucked the cup into your hands before you even thought to ask.

'How bad is it? I mean, ought we get onto the police or something?' Ensconced in his light filled kitchen, tea at his elbow, while the disaster Kate brought spewed out the handset. Such grim pleasure to imagine Gary sinking in a murky viscous sea of it, his very own version of the seep. One hand suspended above the rippling surface, clutching at the phone. Flailing. Gone.

'If the cops are funded as well as everything else down here they'll just write a report and stick it in some file unless handed something concrete to give two shits about. I've been in touch with the local fieries. They were super helpful.'

'Well I can see they charmed your socks right the hell off.' Her disgust was not difficult to read. 'Kate, I'm waiting to hear *in concrete terms* exactly why you're not driving back.'

'Effects. We've found some pretty clear effects.' Or at least, in the face of Lin's enthusiasm they were coming to feel clear. Like astronomers figuring the existence of a planet they could not see: the town *had* to be there, and massive, by how it deformed all around it. 'We're having to work round the edges to start off, but I'm pretty confident more pulling of threads will lead us in.' Well she *sounded* confident which so far as supervisors went was just as good.

Not Gary. Gary knew horseshit when he smelled it—he would not have been lumped with Kate otherwise. 'I see.' Another of those pauses. 'Would you mind passing me to Lin?'

'I can't put Mummy on the phone at this exact second but I'll be sure to say you were asking. Yes, yes, bye Gary.' Quick to hang up while she still had the last word.

And then left on her own, to look around. In the quiet. In surroundings that'd been dandy, something of a treat, until compared to Gary's. Which was about as productive as being envious of the moon.

Besides, Kate was an adult, wasn't she? She could brew her own damn tea if she wanted it so bad. The room had an electric kettle browned with abuse and an assortment of those sad little paper sachets all faded from the sun. Tea, sugar, instant coffee. No aroma left. No mug, either.

Kate had to use the water glass which made it too hot to pick up. Burnt her fingers. The image that rushed through her all of a sudden was of Billy the bright and sinister fireman, Billy reaching ecstatically into a conflagration. His eyes. Kate shook herself sharply, not about to countenance that punk intruding on her sanctuary.

Her ripe fest slunk into her nostrils. Toxins masquerading as beer oozed from her cringing pores, it was so rank she was surprised the headboard's lacquer didn't blister. Chalked a mental note to pop out later for a toothbrush. See if she could scare up somewhere that sold clothes. If not, wouldn't be the first time she laundered in a sink. What did they call it? A whore's bath. That squeezed out a barking laugh.

The cold hissing shower dislodged fragments of memory she could do without; but try telling your brain to be useful, see where that gets you. Each time she found herself torn between turning them over curiously, or lobbing them back into the dark where they'd do no harm.

The strongest impression was heat. A clench of heat. Last night had been on the muggy side before the rain hit, sure, but nothing like this—sweating like she'd been staked out at noon. Blind with it, slithering in sweat. Groping and flinching with her hands while the drunken world swung around, and around, and …

Kate resolutely thrust that one away. Devoted new minutes to giving pits and ass crack a hearty scrub. The unpleasant recollection was not so different to how that dusty pile of notebooks had stung her back at the institute. Little forlorn voices calling to each other in the dark—and if she had to describe being human to an alien, that's exactly how she'd put it.

Must be ever so careful now. Sneaky don't you know. Careful of what? Had *Kate* been sneaky, blundering around in the rain while the others were sleeping? The seep closed in protectively. A manifestation of poor mental health, also a coping mechanism against estrangement. Drunk or sober, Kate was never going to be "fixed" but she had a handle on her own shortcomings.

The shower and the seep: double layers thrown up in the cramped cubicle. Together they seemed to expand its murky boundaries. The ripple glass stall frosted, then toppled away. Kate stumbled, off the vertical.

This was as she had been staggering through the night, she remembered that much. Drunk Kate's world was chaotic, nowhere you would want to visit. Hands and feet numb at the ends of battering limbs. Tried to drink her beer, no *Eric's* beer, only she'd dropped it along the way, and the gesture became a meaty mouth slap. No matter. Could hardly feel the drool either.

The banging started up, out there in the dark. A gush of foreboding welled from the deep lake at the heart of her where the seep rose from lightless waters. Sober Kate could almost see for herself what her alter had witnessed, if she squinted her eyes against the mist.

Only, she simultaneously broke out in a prickling rash of awareness that there was something out there searching for her. She desperately did not want to be found. Not by that. Like a powerless child who believes covering their eyes will hide them Kate wanted to claw her face off and render herself invisible.

Whimpering, hoping to elude notice she began to crawl.

Ought to be wrist deep in mud out here with the rain sluicing down but instead hard pebbled dirt scratched her palms. The door banging. She had to move quickly.

Then a resounding crack as thick skull impacted shower door. 'Ow! Mother*fucker*!'

It was a brand sparkling new headache that brought Kate back to herself. In scrambling to escape a vague terror she had almost gone right through the safety glass. Incandescent flares crazed her vision. They had to be fought, kept from spreading; pass out in the shower and Supervisor Gary would be unsurprised to hear of her ignominious end.

Oh goody: Kate had also sent her molars into the fleshy sides of her mouth. Water pattering to slick hair down over her eyes, across her tongue. Blood and cheap soap taste. This was not her day.

No, there was something else. Had to push free of her misery bubble to hear it. Knocking. A hard aggressive bang-bang on the motel room door. Somebody who felt they had the right to come in.

With partial success she shook her wits into place. Most likely it was the proprietor, complaining she was squandering the flat metallic water. Tank hoarded, precious. Never mind there wasn't a sniff of another customer, they *might* be raising dust just down the road.

Well Kate quickly girt herself in a snaggled beige almost-towel—the type that *almost* goes around, irrespective of girth. The quickest way out of any conversation was to make it too awkward to bear. Not above low tactics such as nudity she swung wide the door.

Static clashed with seep, fit to tear your eardrums as they struggled to cancel one another out. It was only as rabid buzzing flooded the portal that she realised her mistake and the best her scrabbling mind could come up with was, 'Fuck.'

Fireman Billy looked on with bland unsurprise. There was a numbing roar as his weight surged onto the front foot, eager to establish a beachhead. Kate swiftly blocked with a firm arm across the doorframe, no you don't sonny jim, almost lost her towel doing it.

He subsided, not wanting to push past civility just yet. That would spoil the game. His two little mates cringing behind him in their sunglasses, their faces more stable today, broadcasting contempt for her creases and folds.

What did you expect: they were taut youth. So far as their sleek heads were concerned they would exist in beautiful limbo forever. Kate bounced the dual sneer right back, that was part of the game too. Never show so much as a flicker of fear. Not even at her unexpected vulnerability, her humiliating exposure before her enemies.

'Kate!' Billy broke the stalemate, delighted, charmed—never happier than imagining he had the upper hand. 'I've come to take you to lunch.'

'Not up for it.' Her traitorous gut had other opinions, though, loud enough to be heard. It would whine at the feet of anyone who fed it.

'Oh but I insist.' Resist too hard and crack courtesy's scab. How much was the relief of getting hostilities out in the open worth? And there was always the looming danger of the last argument to be subverted, skipped aside. Until you couldn't anymore.

Although capitulation was not in her nature, she nodded and closed the door quietly. Pick your battle. She re-dressed, hating her soiled clinging clothes, hating everything including not having time to towel her hair. The hate would keep. It had a long shelf life.

Lunch it was, all four of them, back at the pub which was the only local offering. Everything as she and Lin had left it. The warm uncertain light falling through stained glass. Sticky hops infused carpet. The same old men fossilised in place by the telly.

The brisk blast of air con to the face was a relief and Kate's mind started to clear. Water dripped shivering down her back. From his station half hidden by thick glassware the owner nodded ambiguous welcome, no smile, and Billy's cronies stared back.

Sam and Sue still wore their fancy sunglasses indoors; the prospect lingered that there were no proper faces behind the blank lenses. Was that what prolonged exposure to Billy's signal-jamming static did? Went for the soft tissue first, the eyes?

They kicked and jostled legs under the table, it was like being stuck at a kindergarten for piranha. Billy capitulated indulgently. 'You guys can go watch the game if you prefer.' Off in a flash, almost upsetting their seats in a flurry of tanned limbs. Kate could only cross her fingers in the hope of seeing one run smack into a wall. Zero interest in what their nominal leader was up to. So why drag them along?

Billy-o conferred overlong at the bar, and at one stage actually pointed across the room at Kate. *Check out my new toy.* He'd look a whole lot less smug with that barstool rammed sideways up his ass.

The generous over-pour he ferried over and set in front of her even smelled expensive, and she accepted with no small pleasure. It might not be possible to empty a man's wallet over a meal but as spite was her witness Kate intended to try.

A quick second trip to fetch his equally brimming schooner—obviously not "double fisting" as the English put it. The logical place to sit was opposite her. Most people hardly think when they array about a table but there's math to it. Rather bafflingly, Billy set down his beer and dragged a chair alongside like they were on a date and could not bear to be apart.

To cover her disquiet Kate sipped. Wine cauterised her damaged mouth, so burningly lovely, oh yes. The rest of her poor abused meat sack was still ringing from last night's adventure and the shower collision, wanted no truck with booze but Billy toasted her so she drank again. Stinging diminished enough for taste: an explosion of liquorice and cigar the owner had stretched to the top shelf for.

'So …' Billy gathered foam off his lip with a chummy smile, no better than a sly wink, humour Kate fancied no part of. The git wanted her for something. She stared back stoically. 'I see you've been keeping company with Mr Platton.' That earned him blankness. 'That's Mr *Eric* Platton.'

The penny hit the floor. 'You mean the caretaker.'

He snorted, the sort of gust a horse might make—horse's ass, anyhow. 'Caretaker. Yeah, sure. If you like. Truth be told, Eric's some crazy bugger who squats out there, communing with the rocks or some shit. Those on high tolerate him 'cause he keeps kids from vandalising the ruin too bad but he's not getting *paid* or anything.'

Kate squashed an urge to defend Eric, who she knew about as well as the jerks surrounding her now. This was deep jerk territory. 'That's … not entirely the story I heard.'

'I'll bet. Look, Kate, since we're onto stories it's important I tell you again what I said out in the bush and this time you should listen. You need to stay away from Pillars Institute. And steer clear of Eric Platton, too. He's not right in the head. That place should be left to moulder, not maintained.'

'Why?'

'There's no point preserving a chunk of history that was rotten inside and out.'

'Didn't look like much to me. A bunch of buildings.' Her nose would grow for that one.

Billy slapped the table, called out to the bar. 'Jack! Hey, Jack?' Apparently the owner's name was Jack, and Kate's memory was rubbish. 'Can we borrow your Da for a minute?

Need a dose of local nous for the visitor.'

'Arse,' Old Dad grumbled from his corner where the handsome feral youths had him and the other old buggers penned in. He showed yellow teeth that must have been false.

'You sure?' Billy sing-songed, like the complete nutsack that he was. 'There's booze in it for you.'

Kate glanced down at her own glass in horror. Almost empty. She had been mindlessly chasing the same lure. Of course, waking up to yourself and being able to *do* anything about it were entirely different animals. Even now her hand brainlessly ferried that same glass to her lips: you're tense honey, here, this might help.

As he shuffled from the corner with the television's blue light flickering over his face Old Dad exchanged a sour look with his progeny—the wordless lingo that passes within families. Kate's heart didn't exactly leap at the sight but ventured a few tentative hops. The denizens of the pub were no friends of the firemen.

Billy-o clapped the older man on the shoulder, blissfully unaware. 'Kate here's been asking about the institute.'

Good Old Dad hawked one up like he was preparing to spit an oyster right on the table. No crossed wires here: as Billy's dogs were to Kate, so was she to this old man, and so on. Anyone outside your immediate circle was no person but a joke, a thing. 'Ask about somethin' else. Nothing good for anyone out there.'

Listening in, owner Jack grunted like bad news was all anyone could expect, especially out here. Only some stray tourist would be addled enough to think it pretty, and only on their way to someplace else.

But it *was* pretty, Kate thought defiantly. So long as happiness in no way hinged on employment, services, or access to liberal schooling. Young families must drain from the population like a sluice opened. The odd retiree might wash up to blow their savings for a decade, but only until medical support became the dealbreaker. Few souls facing mortality wanted to be beyond the reach of an ambulance.

'What *is* out there?'

'Death of ourselves. Who we wanted to be. See, we went off and fought wars all righteous-like, 'cause it was the right thing to do. Come home and find out those who sent us had been doing 'zactly as the other side. Killed us. Killed us dead, knowing that. Took the heart out of the world.'

Mouth tight, his grim point made Old Dad shuffled off to the bar for his reward. Billy watched him go wistfully. The fireman had sunk a lot of warm and fuzzy into the community and wondered why there wasn't better return. 'See? Ask anyone and you'll hear the same. Lotta resentment for what got done in our backyard.'

'Everyone hates the institute. I get that, thanks. But *why*?'

He set his beer down. Earnest time. 'You ever hear of neoliberalism, Kate? Financialization?'

Boys in school played the same tired game: trotting out big words so's they could be Papa Bear and give the little lady an education.

'No? Don't roll your eyes, you ought to know; society's been sucking its flabby teat since the seventies, hoping for just one more mouthful. A fairy tale sold by assholes: money kisses everything better. And those on top give themselves all the breaks while preaching to the masses, "Oh, you're just not up here yet 'cause you ain't working hard enough." Cash, bloody competition and rigged failure allowed to supplant every value—it's the goddamn golden calf all over.'

'Oh. And Pillars?'

'Well the "bad guys" that Jack's Old Dad was sent off to fight had been up to all sorts of nasty tricks hadn't they? Nasty *new* tricks. So when a sack of cash to set up an "institute" landed in their laps the powers that be near pissed their pants with excitement. "Researching health concerns," that's how it was sold. And, you know, sticky issues like consent weren't so much on the table. Not back in the day when there was funding to be spent.'

Billy sat even further forward, pride poking through his disgust. 'But people from around here weren't stupid. The red and the blue got wind, my own station chief, they went up to Pillars together, turned up unannounced. And you know what they found?'

'I have a feeling you're about to tell me.'

'Place was packed with poor folk, immigrants, some trying to get off drugs, some taken out of other institutions. Transients, like your Mr Platton. Transients came out to say hello and they smiled at the officers through lips thick with blisters, mumbled they was trialling "vitamins" or flu remedies. Those that could speak. Others were too burned, inside their mouths, some of them. They'd had stuff rubbed on their skin or into cuts or asked to hold it under their tongue "like a lozenge." And some had straight up vanished with no records to confirm where they'd gone. Got brains and ran off, I can only hope.

'Public outrage saw the institute close its doors before the year was out but wouldn't you know, all those doctors had rich friends. Got themselves shipped off to squeaky clean new careers.'

'Of course they did.'

'See, you're not even surprised. I reckon Jack's Dad had it backward: things were always like this, a world designed to shit on its lowest members, keep them down like animals while the cream, well, they remain untouchable. His generation's tragedy was not being able to shut their eyes to it anymore.'

For fuck's sake—he was practically in Kate's lap now, his excited beery breath gusting across her face. Wouldn't be the first time somebody used politics to slide in. 'If you'll excuse me, I need to visit the ladies.' She had to slip out from under him to escape. Less needing to pee than wash his influence off, gulp some air.

There was a big old picture window in the washroom, which Kate had never been keen on; ventilation be damned, if you could look out you could look in. And what was the point? Not a lot of view to admire as she splashed her hot face at the sink, just the dusty vacant lot behind the pub. Hopeful parking space for the day there might be overspill from out front, but don't hold your breath.

Window on a wasted space dusted with crispy weeds, and likely some scabby feral cats and foxes. Both groups, reservoirs of nasty virus, would love stalking through the thin vegetation, sharp eye on the pub's bins. Threading their way disdainfully between blots of poisoned bait dried into jerky.

And there was one other thing in that tiny wasteland.

In that first squinted glance while towelling her hands Kate thought inexplicably of snowmen, which could not be. Stupid, she was all spun around, it was hotter than hell's balls out there. Not a snowman. It was a rock man, smack in the centre of the lot. Stacked out of what looked like dumped construction rubble.

Scorched grasses waved here there and everywhere but nothing brushed its flanks, drawing back as though squeamish. That lumpy facsimile of a head could have been facing any which way but Kate got the uneasy impression it was locked on, staring intently at the building she stood in.

Of course she recognised it. She had seen the like twice now and they were the sort of thing to stick like indigestion in her looping gut. Still optimistically held out thin runny hope that they might be leftovers from some perverse craft festival—who knows what folk get up to in the country?

Kate was not the type to permit intimidation by a stack of rocks, especially not with a dose of liquid foolishness beneath her belt. She glared back, dizzy and becoming increasingly afraid to look away.

Darkness seemed to crawl in the gaps between the stones. Thicker and more intense the longer she prodded with her dry scratchy eyes, like it went a long way in there. Far deeper than was reasonable. Kate could almost peer in and recognise what was stirring.

The door banged open. Sue, bursting in impatiently to check what was taking so long. At least she assumed it was Sue, given they were in a ladies toilet, but the two were so similar you could never be one hundred percent certain.

'Lunch's on the table,' the girl rapped out. Glasses stared at Kate in the mirror with flat reptilian regard. Wordless scorn for the older woman, her sagging dumpy body—all read as signs of weakness. So much for the commonality of sisterhood.

Kate managed to keep her smiles on the inside. Such a proud ripe young thing but Sue would learn, they all did, to reflect bitterly on adolescent ignorance. 'Scrummy.' Pushing past, Kate exited briskly to get out of line of sight of that window. A glance back as the door slapped shut presented a disturbing glimpse of Sue pressing a lewd kiss to the wasteland window.

Kate's dander was up, and striding back into the bar the vista suddenly clicked, like a magic eye image. As she'd idly noted the bar's high corners were lousy with carved angels, leftovers of the room's more dignified heritage.

Only now Kate saw how every angel faced a window or door with forbidding hands raised. Denying something entry. Their faces looked enraged. And the biggest concentration were clustered toward that vacant lot at the rear of the building.

Catching her gawping Jack winked behind the bar, his eyes like pitted dead marbles, and put a slow finger to his lips. *Sh.* It was not a gesture meant to reassure.

Shaken, she stumbled back to the table to get away, even if it meant returning to Billy. Their meals had indeed arrived, steaming away, but Kate scarcely recalled what they were for.

More wine. Billy had been busy while she was gone and she snatched after it eagerly: more wine would centre her again. He nodded approvingly. 'Plenty more where that came from.'

With tooth grinding effort Kate set the glass down, even knowing her fingers would be on it when attention turned. Amusement writ large Billy settled closer, which she could have done without. 'Kate, I *know* why you're here. I know what you're looking for. I know what Mr Platton's after, too.'

'World peace?'

He ignored her. 'It's not real, you understand? Just some old story. People endured hard lives back then—hell, it's no cakewalk now—and it was like, dreaming somewhere to go allowed them to stay put. Told themselves they could leave someday if they want, just not today.'

'And is that really so bad?'

'False hope?' He laughed, that hard core of meanness. 'I reckon. Plenty of false hope in the house I grew up in, I've seen it firsthand. Buckets of stuff when instead of getting his shit together my Uncle went walkabout. There was some big fight, I think he took up with a cult. But you see, Kate, people can walk out of their life sure enough. If they're assholes enough. I ain't never heard of anyone coming back.'

Kate wanted to demand, *Why are you telling me your sob story?* She'd laugh if she were not already wound into anxious knots.

The ladies room door banged, making them both jump but it was just the she-hound returning to her kennelmate's side back in old bastards' corner. Billy tracked her the whole way. Kate gestured at them. 'And what do your pals believe?'

'Those two. Only thing in the universe they believe in is themselves …' Billy hauled himself to a stop before it went further.

Well, *now* his choice of seat became plain. It was, Kate realised, to keep an eye on his fierce charges. Even in this "safe" setting Billy knew better than to turn his back. Look at them. Laughing too loudly, spreading obnoxiously to take as many chairs as possible, their territory, *theirs!* Twin appreciative snarls. Scarcely in control of themselves.

The displaced seniors huddled against the walls, not daring retreat, which might lead to a terrorised chase. Step lightly, old bean; if you must, go backward to keep line of sight. Predators would be unable to resist the chance to sink their teeth in and shake you all about.

For Kate to shuffle her chair and put her own back to them was a gesture to Billy as much as his vicious mongrels. *See? I'm not afraid. And I've got your measure now, Billy-o. I'm not afraid. But **you** are.* She had always been a competent liar. Still, despite the air conditioning sweat followed water's old path down her spine. If Sam and Sue caught the slightest whiff of fear it would be a short chase.

It may not be his lone reason but Billy was courting her as an ally against those two. Kate smiled, finally, and raised her glass. Idiot.

Loudly refusing to be escorted back to her motel room was one of the most satisfying things she had done all day. It was a close thing, but jelly-legs got her there.

The room was stuffy. Still supposing the forgotten tea might be drinkable Kate sipped and of course it was over steeped and horrible, the opposite of comforting. It a fit of pique she grimaced and flung it at the wall.

The motel proprietor was way ahead of her there—instead of exploding in a starburst of glittering shards the glass merely clunked to the floor. Oh prosaic reality. She had to pick it up, wipe it out with a tissue and return it to its doily. *Think* Kate. Don't just flail about angrily.

Only tipsy, thank goodness, so she still had the means to draw up with a kind of saurian dignity and use her head. First she changed rooms. Gallingly like retreat; she had not even managed to belong to a transitory space for very long, but nothing else for it. The dried wisp behind the front desk was pleased to double-dip, so she'd put a smile on *somebody's* face today.

Appallingly, Kate had barely settled in her new digs before there was a knock at the door. More tentative than Billy's hammering had been, more of an apologetic scratch. She wrenched it open. 'You!'

'Uh, yeah.' Eric trailed Kate back into the room and helped himself to the only chair. That left her the bed. He even perched in the same prissy way as last night: *statue of a curly haired man sitting.*

'How did you know what room I was in?'

'Asked at front desk.'

Kate punched her flat pillow. 'These *fucking* people!' And to his bewilderment, 'Look, I've already changed rooms because Billy the fucking fireman was pounding at my door.'

'Huh. That guy.'

'He didn't seem too fond of you either.'

'Well of course not. I've nothing for him. That's one go to the head of the class kinda guy, he only "likes" folk who can be useful to him.' After a deprecating shrug Eric peered at her more closely. 'Wow. Into the sauce again, huh? Can't believe you got back on that horse so soon.'

'What I ride and when is my own business thank you very much.'

Not too tipsy, eh? In control? Spurred by innuendo it suddenly dawned on Kate that while she'd had the brains to bar Billy, she'd let Eric stroll right on in. Even closed the door behind him. Why? Because he *looked* harmless?

Fogged mental wheels began turning their instinctual analysis of avenues of escape, potential weapons, and how thick were these walls if she had to scream for help? A disproportionate share of female cognition was given over to threat management—just Kate's luck that when she indulged hers became defective. 'What are you holding?' Not wanting to sound nervous.

Eric held it up, waggled it a bit. Clumps of dirt fell to the carpet. 'You don't recognise this?'

'It's a beer can.'

A useless *empty* beer can, drunk Kate piped up from the depths. But she was not entirely right.

'It's not a can.'

'Is this a zen thing?'

'You really don't recognise it?' Eric began extracting something from the mucky lump with tweezering fingers, something Kate definitely did not want to see. Fastidious in his treatment. 'It's a letter.'

A shudder flashed across the surface of her skin like lightning, leaving the core untouched but threatened. 'No, no I think you'll find it's a can. Throw it out.'

Eric rolled his eyes. 'So there I was, finished my laundry and got back to the institute. Started, uh, tidying.' Kate flushed. That ought to have been her job. 'Following the trail of beer cans you left, picking them up, at least I can recycle them. Trail led to the shed. I don't like going in there, isn't a nice place.

Wasn't for storage, see, whatever it looks like.'

'Not unless they were storing nightmares.'

'Funny you should say. It was a quarantine shed.'

'What, for *people*?'

'Got it in one. Your trail of cans went in and I stood there, sweating. Didn't want to follow but I'd started this cleaning up.'

'So you turned around and made a nice cup of tea and lived happily ever after.'

'Didn't smell too good out of the light. Like some yob had cracked the seal on something rancid that ought to have stayed crusted over. And in the corner of the shed there was a hole. Clawed into the mud by fingers. Wasn't there before. *You* dug that hole.'

'Didn't.' No way to prove it, even to herself.

'Went back and got a torch. Instincts were yammering to use my boot an' just shove the soil back in, forget about it. But the beam picked out a glint amid the clots and lumps. So like an idiot I knelt and stuck my arm in, shivering 'though it had to be forty degrees in there at least. At the bottom I found this. There's paper inside.' Eric edited out how he had felt: sluggish, drunk. His brain made stupid and compliant by the heat. Nobody needs the whole unflattering story.

'What does it say?'

He held it out to her.

'You haven't read it? Seriously?'

'Well … you dug it, and I …' A shy look. 'I was too chicken to read it on my own. Especially up there.'

'It's probably a treasure map. You could still toss it in the trash.'

'Like that's going to happen.'

'Fine. You read. I'll be right in here.' All that wine running through her like water. Feeding the great, still lake.

Kate sat longer in the bathroom than she intended. On the loo, twiddling her thumbs, thinking of nothing. She only emerged once she realised a pathology of hiding in bathrooms was brewing. 'Holy shit!'

Eric was clutching his chest, breathing in short whistling whoops. The paper on the ground at his feet. He looked like his heart was splitting.

'Eric!' All that first aid training jammed her circuits in a useless panicked mess. 'Calm down!'

Kate meant herself but he seemed to listen, scrabbling at the armrests of the chair. Could not have been getting sufficient air in those hitchy gasps—otherwise he would have been screaming.

She barked, 'Breathe!' trying to sound like she knew what she was doing. He seemed a lad who appreciated clear instructions. 'Breathe, Eric. One big breath. Come on, you can manage one.'

He got a half in which was an improvement, then bettered it, good lad. Long whoops of air now. Whole body heaving like he had run a marathon.

'For fuck's sake.' Kate subsided on the floor beside the chair, wiping a hand over her mouth. Had he keeled over, how was she supposed to explain that to the hotel proprietor? Or Supervisor Gary?

Eric, thankfully not dead, managed to get enough oxygen to croak, 'Read it.' Then he was up and stumbling to the door, throwing it wide to stand with hands on knees sucking in gusts of the fresher, hotter air. He resembled a trembling old man silhouetted against the light. Kate imagined he looked like his father.

What Eric also looked like was an advertisement to all and passing sundry that Kate had *boys* in her room. Picking up the dirty crumpled paper she snapped, 'Get back in here and shut the door. They'll charge me for guests, and God knows what else.'

The letter read *Dear Mum and Dad.*

She looked up at Eric. 'Are you shitting me?'
He was not.

Dear Mum and Dad

I used to think, and hey it's funny you know, I used to think there was no way out of my old life. Then I thought there was no way out of Pillars. Ha! Before I knew how bad things could get.

The air's always so still here. People talk about what a breeze feels like, puff on each other's faces to try recreate the feeling. It's like nature herself tried to cut us off in revulsion, although nothing natural about how it was done.

I heard about the town from other poor souls at Pillars, it was their favourite bedtime story. A place to escape to. Somewhere you could be happy, and finally know who you were. Of course every fairytale needs a bogeyman. Those were the parts I refused to credit, I needed to believe in the town so very badly.

I told myself the threat of the Seer was the weak justification for staying put, for not seeking paradise. And I mocked them, I actually mocked those poor souls with nothing but misery to their name. I ought to have looked at the eyes. Frightened eyes. Nobody can fake that.

He's real. The town is real but the Seer is too. I haven't seen him yet, not with my own eyes, but the others whisper he's the reason nobody can leave. That he's planning to seal us in for good. They warn me not to look at him if he comes creeping out of his shack. Well I'm going to look, damned if I don't, but so far all that's emerged has been creepy old music.

Don't talk too loud, they whisper. Don't search for a way out. He sees. Somehow, the Seer always sees what we do. The air doesn't move, the music hangs like a reminder he's watching.

I'm still trying to come home. My luck has to change, right, after all this time it has to. Hope you read this someday—I'll even have a little bro now, crazy! Read it to him, too.

Don't forget me.
Love, Ben.

'That's my brother,' Eric said in a trembling hurt voice.
'Yes.'
'That's my fucking brother! When did he write that? How ... I've been at the institute for months! Why this now? Why did you find it? What's so special about you?'
Kate showed her teeth, tired of accusations. 'Nothing. There's nothing special about *anybody*. We're all fools trying to justify our rank in some stupid hierarchy, and for what? To get to kick down and feel better? Big whoop.'
'Is that so.'
'People are all just jerks to me. Equally jerks.'
Eric exhaled hard through his nose, turning to pace in an angry little circuit of the motel room. That he was still putting in effort spoke of the importance of having her understand. 'Not everyone feels like that. *I* don't! When I walked out on my parents I lost everything, now it's like I sprang from a void. How can you belong anywhere feeling like that?'
This was the trickiness of the stranger facing you. They were genuinely *other*, and hard work, not some iteration of the world you already knew. Their lives turned on different pivots.

Theirs was the unfamiliar and the eerie, which is why nobody tries too hard to understand. Theirs is the sharp corners and unstable footing which makes the xenophobic ape inside every human scream its discomfort.

He was still walking without going anywhere, still talking, poor Eric. Patron saint of not holding anything in. Alarmingly it seemed like he wanted to touch her. Perhaps take her hand. 'Maybe it's become normal for people to feel dead inside, to be cut off and alone.'

He did take her hand. It hung dead in his grip. 'Isn't a soul in the world who'd care if I died out there at the institute. What happened to Ben has come around to me and I'll vanish. I need to find my brother. To stop it. So you swear to me, Kate, swear you have absolutely no memory of digging this up.'

Kate jerked her hand back.

'Hey, don't blow up so quick. It's just all so strange, but I believe you.'

Those were not words Kate heard too often. 'If that's true, then stop asking, ok?'

'I believe you were sauced, and you honestly don't remember.'

Prickling needles of suspicion. '*You* said you don't like to drink at the institute.'

Eric looked uncomfortable. 'That part of your recall's pretty sharp, for …'

'For a drunk?'

'I didn't mean ...'

'Yeah, you did. The institute.'

He sighed. 'It's easier when I'm the one being magnanimous. Look, odd things happen when you drink too much out there. It's why I don't have as much trouble with delinquent kids as I probably should. But, you know, nothing tangible, nothing like *letters*.'

'When you say odd, do you mean odd clown odd? Odd socks?'

He rubbed at his non-existent goatee, eyes still on the letter. 'I'd better show you.'

Chapter Six

Tourist

In a grand tradition somewhere between bloody minded and foolhardy, they set off for Pillars Institute the next morning. The weather was again so arid Kate could feel mucus membranes threatening rupture. The irritation provoked constant snuffling.

Crawled up inside you like a fever, that heat. Sluggish and thick. How delicious, though, to be out doing exactly what fireman Billy warned against. Really put a sparkle in her inflamed eye.

'I don't like to drink,' Eric confessed, breaking her introspection with his own.

And hadn't the shy caretaker scrubbed up well, although the day's sweaty clambering about promised to put paid to that. Eric led the way on foot from where the roaring bus had disgorged them, not bothering to glance back, although Kate did.

Through hot billowing exhaust a few schoolchildren pressed against smeared glass as the vehicle lumbered away. They had recognised Eric, that much had been obvious. Not that they made any twitch to acknowledge either adult plonked in their midst. Merely stared in peculiar listless silence as the bus jolted along, knocking against one another like dolls lined up on a shelf.

Creepy little sods.

'I mean, not *drink* drink. Never saw any drunk do nothing admirable or clever.'

'Tell that to your fancy new letter,' Kate griped, already falling behind. He still clutched it and that stupid beer can too, so fervently his nails were as white as hers. 'Drunk Kate dug that shit up.'

'I was including myself.'

'Well be sure you don't drown in the deluge of admirable cleverness you get off sober folk.'

'Kate, people aren't always as horrible as you make them out to be.'

'Oh yes they are.' Awkwardness tugging between them. 'As soon as you give them a chance, they are.'

'Just throwing it out there: your attitude may have some bearing on that.'

Kate's view was predominantly of Eric's ass. Dry crunch crunch following his boots up a trail only he could see. The dapples of shade they crossed encouraged chartreuse blowflies to alight on bare skin, a lick of the feet, just enough to feel shivery and gross and she thought *thank goodness Lin took the car*. Lin would hate this. Loudly.

Today was a sight less organised than the previous hike. Eric and Kate both had bottled water and thin service station sandwiches in plastic bags that rustled as they trudged, hers tied to her handbag. If Kate was prepared to believe Eric, he managed this commute often enough without falling off the map. Were she wrong, well, sorry fireman Billy, there's mud in her eye.

Eric did not need to save his breath for walking. So far as Kate was concerned all fit people could go to hell. 'Anyways, the first couple of weeks out here on my own were pretty depressing. Wasn't sure I'd made the right choice, chasing after my brother. Couldn't be sure of a lot of things.'

'How much were you expecting to turn up, anyhow? The site's so old and shoddy and ruined.'

'You wouldn't believe what gets left when people clear out of a workplace and stop giving a crap. The second the paycheques stop it's down tools. See ya later.'

Now she was thinking about it, that's exactly what would happen at her workplace. It would be sealed up and left a time capsule to bland corporate existence.

'Know what cleaners found while emptying a storeroom in Maryland? Smallpox. I shit you not—sixty-five years after its supposed eradication, here's smallpox, shoved in some shitty box and forgotten about.'

'Ok, pro tip: you do *not* want to share that story with Lin.'

'Yeah, she doesn't seem to handle germs and stuff.'

'What can I say? Her body is a temple.'

'Well, discovery is sometimes about opening the right boxes.' Eric stopped. 'What's that noise?'

His hearing was better than hers. Kate fumbled in her handbag, only now catching her phone's distinctive rasp. 'Ah, speak of the devil. Excuse me a mo.' She walked off for a bit of privacy. 'Lin, how's your day going?'

'I'll be swinging back to you, and you're not going to believe who I dug up. *Carol Meyersen.*'

'Is she a celebrity? I'm not good with pop culture.'

The eye rolling was audible. 'Miss Carol had the dubious pleasure of growing up on the hideous farm of ick. Only twelve when they packed it in but she remembers as clear as day, which frankly I wouldn't want to, *if* I ever made it out of therapy. One tough cookie, this girl. I'm telling you Ms K that farm is *not* right.'

Lin coughed into the phone, cleared her throat which had Kate holding it away with a grimace. 'So my investigation's been a success all 'round. Wish I could feel happier about it. Where are you at?'

'Ah …' Kate glanced about, short on wins to report. 'I'm standing right next to our mate from the other night, actually.'

'That caretaker guy with the hair?'

'No, the creepy rock pile. But Eric's taking me back to the institute to do some more looking today.'

'Whoa, wait, hold up. *Kaaa-te.*'

Instantly on her guard. 'What?'

'Say his name again for me.'

'What? No. Why?'

'OH MY GOD YOU SLEPT WITH HIM!'

Kate put her hand over her flaming face, appalled by how loud that sounded. Surreptitiously checked Eric remained at minimum safe distance. 'Lin …'

The other woman could scarcely get words through her glee. 'Don't you try lying to me, I *know* when a doodle's been schnoodled.'

'Sh, shut up! I'll do anything if you stop saying doodle.'

'Give me some juicy detail or I swear it'll be the first word out of my mouth when I see you guys.'

'He just wanted a shower, all right, with actual plumbing and seeing as I had a room and all …' Kate trailed off. Why *had* she slept with Eric?

Reasonable enough to assume two mature adults could be in proximity without doing the nasty. Perhaps it had been a misguided attempt to reward, he had helped so much. Recalling now with chagrin how little Eric had been into it, either. They both had their own obsessions that hardly admitted a new player. Not this late in the game.

'Look, Eric's coming, I'll talk to you later.'

'*I'll bet he is you sly doodle-loving …*' Kate almost splintered the phone hammering disconnect, and smiled a little too brightly at approaching Eric.

Ignoring her hysteria, he was just pleased to be smiled at. 'Was that really Lin? What, she magically phones whenever you mention her?'

'No, this is new. Normally she calls when I'm on the toilet.' Shoved to the bottom of her handbag the phone buzzed and buzzed. She could almost hear Lin's cackle.

Kate cleared her throat and gestured at the pile of rocks. 'We, ah, got spooked by this in the dark. Thought it was a person.' Light of day revealed the cairn to be less anthropomorphic but no more pleasant. Wasn't illumination supposed to bring sanity?

'Don't blame you. The stink off the bloody thing gives me a migraine.'

Now he mentioned it her offended nostrils were trying to shrivel away, like they could drag her whole face along. 'What maniac built them?'

'Them?'

'There are definitely more than just this one. I've seen two by a weird gate dropped into the middle of nowhere, and another down by the pub. Like they were guarding the place.'

'Or watching.' Eric frowned, a sort of quick animal fright rippling from him to her and back again. 'Don't you feel like it's looking back at you? I always assumed a local kid put this up. One of their dares.'

A slow, sly smile began to creep across Kate's face. She did not like being spooked—it provoked her into being showy and violent. 'Well perhaps they won't mind if we wreck this one, then.'

She began to kick at it vengefully; not the right shoes for the job, but needs must. Rocks slithered off the sides and the stench intensified as though she'd cracked into a vault: sour, pissy. It rolled over them in a wave that sent both stumbling back, gagging, the air *stinging* their exposed skin. *Fuck*, Kate thought, dimly aware that this would make a terrible last moment.

The rich gold sunlight seemed to pale, washing out, losing force. And the droning ever-opportunistic flies died right out of the air to litter the ground around their feet. Kate had no doubt that had they not been larger more complex organisms it would be her and Eric down there too.

Then it dissipated, unable to hold itself together. Kate retched, grateful for the swift resumption of bright hot light that seemed to be steaming the taint off her. 'Gah! Why would someone fill it with piss? Smells like a goatful of piss died in there.'

'I guess … I guess some kind of initiation or something? Schoolkids force each other to come up here sometimes.'

'If that came out of a teenager they need their kidneys scoured with bleach. I am not hanging around here waiting for my face to melt off any longer.' Although with no sense of direction she needed Eric to indicate which way to go. 'I can't believe kids come out here for fun.'

'It's not shits and giggles, that's for sure. I still remember my first few nights: couldn't settle, like ants under my skin, and this was before I knew anything about the place. Has this *feel*, you know? I found myself getting up to tramp about every hour, burning through batteries for no good reason. And boozing was how I'd seen others fill bored moments. Most popular pastime at university, killing brain cells; ironic considering how expensive it is to attend.'

Kate blew sweaty hair off her face. 'You got drunk as some kind of *experiment*?' The polar opposite of how she stumbled in: blind and raving and ignorant, every time.

'Tipsy. I got myself tipsy as an experiment. Not balls-out blotto like you were, that was just crazy.' Fortunately for Eric's tender ears the downhill slope was too steep for reply.

In the dark Kate must have been too wired to notice the gradient, or perhaps she'd run a more circuitous route but now even Eric had to conserve puff. From up there the rock pile had had a great view of the institute. Right until she kicked it to pieces, and Kate grinned wishing she could do it all over again.

Stumbling to the bottom they surveyed Pillars Institute's shabby clearing for themselves. What a place. Eric was not wrong about the ambience. The sagging structures still housed despair that resisted being baked out by the sun's onslaught.

While Kate gasped like a dying thing Eric stretched arms above his head, inviting the air to scorch all the way down to his lungs. You could tell it was something some long-ago gym instructor had taught. 'I sure won't be indulging again. Leave that to the kids.'

'So you're scared to loosen up out here but happy to use schoolchildren as your guinea pigs?' She was beginning to empathise with the blank looks he had drawn on the bus.

Eric threw his hands up. 'Like there's any way I can stop them! I have to sleep occasionally, get food, take a shit. I know what I've told you about my life sounds pretty dramatic smashed together into one story, but that isn't how it's been. I mean, listen. What do you hear?'

Nothing. The faint susurrus of leaves overhead. No intent or malice to it, Kate reminded herself, rubbing her arms. Just the geometry of wind given voice. Absolutely no reason to keep twisting to look over her shoulder.

'That nothing's been the theme music of my days. I sit here twiddling my thumbs in the silence hoping nothing'll happen and desperately hoping it will. Brush my teeth, pick up trash with the tongs, paint walls until the paint's holding 'em together. Seriously, nodding politely to the corner store cashier is a big event in my calendar, something I spend time getting ready for.'

'Is she pretty?'

'After coming so far, it's terrible to want to wait safe in the quiet forever holding my breath.' Discarding diffidence Eric lifted his head at looked straight at her with shining black eyes. 'But they're bad things, Kate. Bad things happen out here.'

'Like during your "experiment."'

'I might write it off as a bad dream only I don't think I was sleeping. Dreams are a process for clearing mental junk but if it chokes, all the nastiness that needs deletion starts piling up. Basically your brain sours from proximity to this place.'

'Ok, ok. I'd not be adverse to a smidge of comfort over honesty if you can manage.' Oppression gazed down at her from the buildings. Eric was stirring badness. She could do with a glass of wine but this was the worst place for it.

Eric's shyness returned, glancing down and away. Kate had to admit it was refreshing not to be the most awkward. 'Sorry. Here, I really don't think I can. Come on. Over this way's where I dug up Ben's letter.'

Bad luck, huh. Against what remained of her better instincts Kate followed him to the shed. Standing in the glare outside made it tricky picking out particulars in the cramped dark space, and she was not going in there. Tried for some levity. 'Well it's a fairly ordinary shed. I don't see any smallpox.'

'Ordinary for some gardening tools, maybe. Not for how these grim sons of bitches used it.'

Kate bent to peer through the doorway and a wave of prickly rage swept in. You could not even stand under that low roof.

'They locked ill people in here? I can't exactly see them getting better.' Only worse. Sinking.

The sole consolation to be so burning febrile inside your skull as they stretchered you across the clearing, stumbling and grunting beneath the burden, sky whirling, that you had no idea where they were sticking you. 'I thought scientists took some kind of oath.'

'You're thinking of medical doctors. Bunches of them end up stepping way beyond the "don't be an a-hole" line, too. The institute liked to spread the misery so they made sure to jam newbies in quarantine for a bit when they rocked up here wondering where they were. An instant, brutal taste of the worst so they'd remember to stay in line.'

His brother, Kate had to keep reminding herself. *Every time he speaks of the institute he's talking about his brother, who was here. A kid, for Chrissake.*

'I actually found the checklist for handling incoming patients. Zero concern for their wellbeing, ten out of ten for preventing the introduction of fleas and sniffles. Reducing variables in the population was a priority. This one researcher, she'd crossed out every instance of "population" and written "the herd."'

Eric stroked his chin fitfully, still yearning for that beard. 'In my not-dream I was in here. This shed.' He swallowed, craning toward the darkness as though searching for his lost carefree cheer.

How many folk would have the spine to come back and confront what so unnerved them, staring in? Perhaps more the hallmark of obsession than bravery.

'I was small. Know how you're vulnerable that way in dreams, all the rational adult stripped away? Small and crying in that cobwebby dark. Not *because* it was dark, gone so far past that. I'd been shoved in with others. People who'd been nice to me. Wasn't so bad when we were all crowded but now I couldn't find them. Didn't know where they'd gone. And that *aloneness*. Being left behind ...

'Had I been awake I'd have known instantly it was a dream. First the reassuring fingers; grownup hands, big enough to promise they had the chaos encompassed somehow; they stopped patting my hair, 'though I clutched after them my own hands closed on *nothing*. Should have been there but weren't.

'Next blink, suddenly no more jostling at my shoulders, no more humid mouths sucking up my air. Same time those voices, those kind voices telling me *sh it's going to be ok*, receded like they were on some high speed travelator getting swept away.

'Happened so *fast*. Inexplicable, unnatural and—ok, scary, massively scary. Happened faster than real folk can move and the cramped shed was locked, knew it was, I'd pounded on the door. Screamed myself bloody for them to come back.

'Even thought for a second I caught an echo of answering cries coming from far away, with a thin crackle behind. And music, of all things. Tinny strings of real old fashioned music. But then nothing. *Nothing*.

'Got in a right flap hammering on the walls I could reach: Boom! Boom! Until I was near deaf and rattling in my arms, but nobody came. The space so small, nowhere to go. And I just kept groping around, crying, 'Where did you go?' hearing it come back broken off the walls. Until I woke. If that's the term. Was standing right here, staring in.'

With a grimace Eric shuffled back. Swivelled to face Kate but never put his back to that doorway. Wise. 'Can imagine how I felt when I came to my senses. Took a while to return to me, the self I've made, a grownup able to take care of business. Layers coming back that I hadn't known could be stripped off. That was pretty much the worst part. Feels like I never really came right, even to this day. Pull something up by the roots, even if you replant it'll not grow the same.

'Anyways, tossed the booze and stocked up on coffee 'til my heart was aching—didn't want to sleep for a week. Carried on 'til I keeled over.' A tremulous smile. 'Strictly a one beer man, now.'

No stranger to enduring the odd bad night, Kate still had to swallow with a dry click before she could speak. 'That's a hell of a brainfart. It doesn't have to *mean* anything; other than this shed is horrifying and we ought to keep our backsides out.'

Didn't the shed call to curiosity, though, with a dark siren pull that had her swaying on her feet. Tidal forces on the still lake at her core. Pretend pragmatism all you want Kate but you can feel it.

'Right here's where I reckon it started for the institute. Something slipped in that they couldn't squash or quarantine, and it proliferated through the populace like wildfire.'

So this was how it felt to wear Lin's skin: shivery and gross. 'A disease?'

'Huh, they could've stopped that. I'm talking an idea. The desperate belief there was somewhere to go. A bunch of patients and at least one researcher vanished in the month before Pillars got shut down. I've got memos complaining of runaways, experiments interrupted and so on. Murder charges were even bandied about when shit really splattered, 'though it'd never stick without bodies so I reckon that was the locals getting nasty about lighting a fire under the departing scientists. Reckon those folk went missing from quarantine here, broke out of the shed somehow. Some of them, anyways.'

Spooky yarns around a campfire. Only this was searing daylight, making it even harder to mask unease. Kate shuffled twitchily back from the shed, too, not wanting to be first on the buffet should it reach out. 'Ben?'

'After finding his letter I really think so.'

'One of the first questions I got stuck on was why anybody would come out here.' She bit her thumbnail. 'Perhaps the escapees didn't want to go, so much as they were driven to get out of Pillars the only way they could.'

Eric looked dubious, although with Kate ruminating so fiercely he hardly wanted to contradict. 'Not sure the town was like that. Folk seemed to really want to go, like fairyland and heaven all mixed. Come have a squiz at these.' He strode across to the office that time forgot, tongs clanking.

Kate trailed and was almost bulldozed over as he clomped back out toting one of the dusty notebooks. 'That's your book? I thought they were old.' Not much of a detective—she had to admit Lin was doing far better.

'Well, yeah, the *books* are. I'm just using them, all this free stationery lying about. Had my parents' work to build on, been collating any relevant hints I dig up. Started noting graffiti too 'fore I paint it over. Thought it'd be neat in case the cops get to charge somebody's folks for damages, but once they were in the same book I could see how it all related.'

'Come again?' Was Eric off the deep end?

'Over here. Want you to get an idea what Pillars was like.'

Eric walked her across and slapped the siding of a structure so sunk it looked like it was flinching, expecting more abuse. 'This was the bunkhouse. Boys and girls separate, supposedly very proper, but isn't a stellar track record for places like this.'

Easy to imagine. Huddled under your inadequate blanket, hearing the heavy creaking step. Waiting for the weight to settle on the end of your bunk. Praying it'd be somebody else's turn tonight, even if you go straight to hell for wishing it. All ears pretend not to hear in the dark. At breakfast nobody will meet your bruised eyes.

'Bunkhouse walls were so poorly insulated they called it the fever mill. Of course patients didn't dare let on they were sick, case they got sent to quarantine. Glassy eyed and gone, shaking to pieces. Just smile, smile. Up here, this end of the bunkhouse one of the researchers started staying up some nights. I have her notes.'

Eric flipped through pages. '*The subjects fall quiet if I come near. I have to skulk. They whisper of a town. What town? It can't be near this forsaken place—beneath these muttering trees is where misery comes to be forgotten.*

'*I can't get the looks on their thin faces out of my mind. Not even when I close my eyes. Can't …* The rest of that one's illegible. But at this very same end of the building I found a kid's graffiti once, it said, T*here's a way through. I'll make them tell if I must. I'll grind them in the fever mill.* You see? No way any kid couldn't known what the bunkhouse was called. It's like the letter. Messages breaking through.'

'I'm not normally a woman of strong opinions, but I would *not* want to meet the person who wrote that.'

'Guess she got shitty at being shut out.'

Kate thought of the dull eyed poppets on the bus. Exhausted was how they'd seemed. Beaten by dread of life before they'd even fully entered it. The perfect conduits, perhaps, for a time.

'Once the correlation 'tween old and new got obvious I got worried. Went and spoke to a few of the teachers. The local kids who sneak out here, they don't do so well. Generally only takes one from each class for the lot to learn, thank Christ, so only need to stress about the newbies. Vulnerable kids who reckon they've got something to prove.'

Kate knew all about those kids. Looked like Eric did, too.

'Remembering growing up in the yard gives me acid, even now. Take risks when you're on the margin; least until you get let in, or give up and accept it as your place. What kills me is the other kids take advantage of that, they *let* 'em come here. Like every now and again this place needs a sacrifice.'

True to the spirit of Pillars to be shivering in the dark. Hoping another gets chosen, just leave me alone. And if you can *make* that happen …

Kate frowned, a patented disgust. 'Human children are basically monsters. Hardwired for cruelty and exclusion, even when they don't think they're doing anything wrong.'

Eric barked with laughter, the tension cracking and flaking off. Kate may not be as charming as Lin but she had her moments. 'And what's your recommendation? Beam back to the 1940s and birch sin out of them? Set orphans to work in chimneys and mines?'

'How did you even know what school your vandals came from?'

'Only the one school here, Kate. And it was one of the teachers came to me in the first instance, she'd had a smidgin of a disaster. Little string bean by the name of Alex. New to the area, of course. Teacher, and Alex, and Alex's outraged middle class folks, the local police sergeant and a partridge in a pear tree, all hammering on my door. Lucky me. A proper invasion, I heard them arguing all the way down the hill.'

'What was the disaster?'

'Turned out Alex'd started screaming in class.'

Actually it started as fairly innocent hiccupping, but teacher was already on guard with this group. She had found the rural students easy enough except that every once in a while one would tend to plummet. Not every class, or every year. Not often remarked on. She'd grown sick of hearing *kids aren't perfect, just teach the ones you can.* How did that fix the problem!

It occurred the same way each time. Grades dropped off. No interest. Sullen. Physical changes, which were hard to pin down but so far she'd characterised muscle loss, hair loss, decreased attention to grooming which normally peer pressure moderated.

Bright futures cut short, some of them. So markedly you could see benefits, government housing, until they ended their grey days sitting in a room staring at nothing. Hearing only the pulse of blood in and out.

Some claim the genius who will save the world has already been born, but so poor they'll never get their chance. To that the teacher silently added *not on my watch*. Since nobody local would lend an ear the rebel inside had sent tap water samples to an old uni pal to test for lead.

Now here sat Alex, head down in the classroom trying not to be seen while tiny high pitched sounds squeezed out. Teacher moved fast between the desks but by the time she reached him Alex was all out bawling, with the rest staring. Preschool had been the last she'd seen its like, which she quit with damaged hearing. The onslaught was a tad unnerving, to say the least.

Her comforting must have been a little rusty because Alex seized her sleeve, his fingers like ice which jolted her even through the fabric and it was well over thirty in the classroom. Enough to lull them all into a quiet stupor before this happened.

The boy began gabbling up at her a mile a minute with snot running down his face, the words running together, took her a moment to tune in. '... bone fingers, yellow old bone poking out of the rock, even smaller than mine, a little *kid's* fingers, made me sick to look at an' I knew I shouldn't touch but they couldn't be real, had to be a trick why else would they send me stupid to think they actually wanted to be my friends so I touched and they made my hand so *cold* and a little kid voice came crying out of the stone it wanted to come through so bad didn't want to die it's still crying missus please *please* make it stop!'

All the other students had abandoned chairs and crowded the other side of the room by this stage, as far away as they could get. A sea of eyes bugging out, like calves about to stampede on their springy little legs. Reality *shifted*. Spilling teacher off, and once sliding good luck clawing your way back.

'Come on, Alex.' She lifted him by his elbow. She had to separate him which wouldn't do him any favours later but she teetered at the brink of losing control of the lot of them. Delivered the boy into the care of nurse, a kind faced retiree-volunteer, while she undertook the unenviable task of phoning Alex's parents.

Even in the evening when all the students had gone and Alex packed into his parents' car, teacher couldn't stop worrying. Figured the boy must have dozed in the sullen heat and had some kind of nightmare. She already knew the move had been stressful: families didn't end up out here when prospects were rosy.

The rap on her office door caught her off guard, she had thought herself alone in the building. The echoing halls usually gave company away long before you saw it. But the guilty faces peering around the door belonged to Sean and Baz, two of Alex's classmates.

Her nerves tightened at those hangdog expressions and she wished Mr Seng who shared the office were here. Even though four together could never fit in the tiny room, not without tossing a few filing cabinets into the corridor. Numbers spread bad luck around.

'Sean. Baz. Come in.' She folded her hands on the desk to still them. 'Do your parents know you're here?'

'S'posed to be at footy,' Sean mumbled, neither boy daring to meet her eye. They weren't going to get to business without help, which she provided despite her misgivings.

'Will you tell me what this is about?'

Now they were on the verge of blubbering although it was a very different kind to what she had seen in class today. Sorry at being found out, she'd bet. 'It's Alex. We made him do an initiation. Up at Pillars.'

'What do you mean, "initiation?"' Difficult to keep her tone level. She nudged the tissues across her desk closer to the boys.

They elbowed one another until the weaker, Baz, copped the duty. Mumbling low enough into his chest as to be inaudible.

'I can't hear you.'

'He had to steal booze. And, and spray his name backwards. At night. Texted us selfies to prove the whole thing.' Baz proffered his phone miserably. 'I don't want these anymore.' Began to wheeze, tears slipping free.

Teacher turned to Sean. 'And your phone?'

'…'

'Pardon?'

'I smashed it!'

'You smashed it. I see.' Teacher didn't, but remained closemouthed as she transferred the series to her phone and deleted them from Baz's tender clutches. She felt terrible thinking how excited Alex must have been to get these two kids' numbers. She already knew the only other contacts on his phone were his parents.

'Both of you head on home. You've done the right thing coming to me with this, but I think you both know you did wrong by Alex. I'll be speaking to your parents.'

Once they had stumbled out, a tissue apiece, she was free to put her face in her hands. Teaching could be so rewarding, it could bring such joy and pride. Other ones, knowing children of all people could be so fucking mean spirited hollowed her out.

At least it was Friday. She gave herself permission to grab a bottle of chardonnay on the way home and cry it all out tonight.

It was not until teacher went through the images that she realised the police would be needed.

Eric folded his arms. 'Landed me in a real hot mess. The circus rolled up here expecting to discover fingertips in stone—a dead body, in other words.

'Know what they found? Go on, I'll let you guess. The tag ends of fuck all. A tad satisfying from where I sat in the back of the cruiser, not that I got any kind of apology when they finally came to let me out. Wasn't even an empty bottle where Alex says he left it up by that pile of rocks which shows the kid had guts. I'd not be poking around there in the dead of night.

'If not for the happy snaps it was like he was never here. Teacher was kind enough to show them to me on her phone while the rest were wandering about yelling at each other. Took the opportunity to forward them to myself because I'm sneaky like ze fox.'

Getting to see them meant waiting around while he messed with his decrepit brick of technology, trying to get it to boot. 'You'll need to be quick. Isn't much battery, normally charge it when I do my shopping.'

Kate winced at the first photo of the series. Alex giving the screen an awkward thumbs up, trying on a smile that did not touch the edges. Late to puberty the bucktoothed lad radiated the sort of soft-mouthed desperation that got bullies salivating. If worse events had not intervened, this photo would have been destined to cruel circulation forever.

'Ah, and these are of the so-called "rum theft." Lot of bluster from the bottle-o that Alex flashed ID and paid, seemed like a nice kid, only it was obvious the cashier only cared about clanging the till. Sergeant reckoned it was the worst photocopied ID he'd seen in a long line of 'em.'

'I'm kind of surprised his parents let this investigation run on.'

'Alex's Mum never said boo but she got this tight little mouth this part of the saga. Sure as rain he lifted the cash from her purse, not wanting to *actually* shoplift; poor trapped rabbit, hardly knowing which jump was the lesser evil.'

The staged theft photos were actually kind of genius. Had it been an art project the school would've been handing out scholarships instead of a criminal investigation.

'Ah, and here are the "fingers." Doesn't look like much, hey?'

Kate had to agree, you would only think "fingers" if somebody had primed you to do so. She was more concerned with Alex's face. There was nothing tangible but as the sequence went on she noticed a change in the boy's hopeful unformed expression.

He became paler. Pinched looking, as though a pained old man's expression were trying to squint through. And more often his eyes shifted. Instead of staring down the barrel to convince those other boys by sheer will to like him, he was searching the surrounding dark.

Kate found herself wishing for a more powerful flash. Humped indistinct shapes swam behind the boy, he could have been at the bottom of the Marianas Trench.

'I thought he was doing his dare alone?' She tapped a finger on the blurry figure in the background. Eric peered over her shoulder.

'Rocks.'

She snorted a laugh: the exact same mistake again. Lin would be so proud. But Eric was frowning at the phone, and twisting this way and that to reconnoitre the site around them.

'What's up?'

'It's wrong. That's not where it belongs.'

'It's not?'

His eyes, too close to hers, were wide, freaked out. '*Look*. The kid, he's standing near the quarantine shed. The pile of rocks shouldn't be anywhere near him.'

Kate's stomach contracted in a queasy foetal knot. Poor Alex's haunted face, half turned to stare over his shoulder, eyes glassy with rum he had not wanted or enjoyed. A doomed expression.

Eric accepted the phone back, nodding as she wiped her hand on her leg. 'Not nice, is it? Reckon it was a mistake dragging that poor kid back out here to show them where he'd seen his "fingers." Poor little bastard went into hysterics, like his brain was broken and had forgotten how to do anything but scream. Voice was just a series of raw honks by the time they left. Idiots. Were never gonna find anything. I'd already painted over Alex's graffiti.'

Kate felt a stab of disquiet, which did not crop up often with Eric but: Surprise! Unsafe anywhere! 'You hid it.'

'Isn't like that! Figured it might be better for him. There's not a lot "normal" about being a young lad, Kate, boys are pretty much a mess all the time. And next stop for Alex's carnival was going to be the emergency room, get his blood tested for toxicity after that shoddy rum he'd been swigging. All those people around him on sharp lookout for someone to blame, and since I'd disappointed ...' He sighed. 'Not that it did him a lot of good in the end.'

'That sounds not great.'

'Phoned teacher later in the week to check on Alex. Inadvertently helped myself to her number along with the photos so might as well use it. Think she might have been annoyed normally, but bigger things to be upset about: Alex went home and tried to clip his fingers off with his father's garden shears.'

'He what?' Ordinary children did not do that. Only the seriously disturbed. Close her eyes and there was Alex's pale doomed face, mouth trembling with pleas unsaid, turning to look over his shoulder at what loomed behind him.

'Apparently his parents found him standing out in the yard in a daze. Dad didn't keep his tools sharp, maybe not much call when they lived in high density.'

'Fuck.'

'So far as I know he hasn't come back to school. Teacher hasn't seen him. None of his class either, 'though I'd doubt they'd do anything but run the other way if they did.'

The unfairness of it made Kate clench up. She had to unstick her jaw to speak. 'The graffiti. What did Alex's graffiti say? I'm assuming you wrote it down before your big coverup.'

Already had his thumb marking the place. Eric opened the page with sadistic deliberation—that was the thing with sour news. It demanded sharing so you could rub some of the attendant bad luck off onto other people. 'In real big letters covering the whole side of the fever mill he wrote "DON'T LET THE SEER HEAR." Over and over.'

'The Seer? Like in your brother's letter.'

'Wasn't even the best of it. *That* I could paint over. Down here. Way down the bottom like he didn't want anyone to see. Tiny writing, actually scratched into the wood. Doesn't that look like it was done by little bone fingertips?'

Kate knelt. The message was read with the fingers as much as the eyes. *"She broke it in half and it was full of old blood, flakes dropping like ash. It's how he's been listening."*

An outline of stones not quite invisible enough beyond Alex's shoulder. The boy's bulging, turning eye. Tongues of red spilling across the white. Cracked open, the rankness of piss.

'Oh God. Oh God, oh God.' Abandoning subtlety Kate upended her handbag right there in the dirt, keys, wallet and change going flying.

'What are you doing, Kate, all your stuff ...'

'In the rocks. Piss in the rocks. And blood—he makes things with bits of himself in them, see—sometimes it's pee, sometimes—and then he can hear you!'

Yes, there it was. The lurking tumour. The little figurine. She stamped her heel and its loathsome face broke apart with a marrow rich snapping. Ground the bulbous body into fragments. What tumbled out, thick with char, was a burnt finger.

CHAPTER SEVEN

INTRUDER

The door whammed and Lin burst in like everyone's birthday at once. Blithely swanning by Kate having a coronary and Eric who nearly leapt through the wall. 'Hooray, I come bearing aid! Snacks, toothpaste; you should probably tell front desk not to give out your room number. Oh. Why, *hello* Eric. Fancy. Seeing. You. Here.'

Kate fell on a bag, desperate to forestall further commentary. Even before opening it her heart of hearts knew there'd be no wine: Lin loved unspoken points as much as the stabbing kind.

What the bag *did* contain was a baffling array of pot noodles. Little sodium bombs that ought to have sent Lin's clean living alarm through the roof. Too much would mummify you from the inside out.

Kate turned one of the rattling Styrofoam pots over in her hand—bad for the environment too! —considering demanding 'Who are you and what have you done with Lin?' when the printed font caught her eye, so *very* close to "doodle." Mortified she stuffed it away while the taller woman smirked.

Kate was normally sharper, but the flurry of humour and interaction was staggering, like a clout to the head. She and Eric had been crouching silently indoors for hours. Stewing in their unease. Hesitant to use the word *hiding* but drawn curtains in the middle of the day did that for them.

Kate had whiled away the time staring at the floor and hopelessly craving her flat. Her instincts were to burrow and her home a contained world, completely under control. There, any threat could only come one way, through the door—or perhaps the phone, but wouldn't be the first she'd thrown out the window in an angry fit. Her fingers unconsciously stroked the fragmenting map in her pocket. Was it wishful thinking that they tingled, imagining a connection to the sketch's more permanent twin on her benchtop? A little piece of home.

Eric had it worse. Mr Feelings faced having to go *back* to Pillars at some point. He gnawed his cheek and wrung his fingers but having come so far he'd hardly abandon the search for his brother. What else did he have to lose?

Their uncovered artefacts were displayed on the chipboard motel table. At first Lin seemed to take no more than a cursory glance while scanning for somewhere to deposit the rest of her burdens. 'Oh, you broke your little dollie! So sad, I'll bet. Hey, and you found some nasty old beer can to bring home, good on you. And … a finger. That's a finger!'

Lightning review of Kate's hands, Eric's, even her own in case the world's nastiest magic trick had been pulled. Then, as only the manifestly confident can Lin refigured, raising an eyebrow at the guilty pair. Here came the voice of reason. 'It isn't real, is it? Bleugh! Explanation in ten seconds starting now or I call the police.'

'Hey, I wanted the cops,' Eric protested. Being jammed in the back of a patrol car had not been as instructive as it should have.

They both turned to Kate and she rubbed her face tiredly: yes, yes all my fault. Tide stirred within but no seep, more was the pity. 'How crazy do you want to get?'

'So it's a contest now. Because you will not even put a dent in my day.'

Challenge accepted. 'You were right, fireman Billy *didn't* pluck that doll off the ground. And as it turns out, body parts are a signature gift of some pal of his.'

'There was a finger in it all this time? Excuse me, I'm gonna go wash my hands.' She returned. 'So who's the pal?'

'Some asshole calls himself "the Seer."'

Kate got no further because Lin went the colour of old stone. Her long legs gave way and Eric leaped from the chair just in time for her to sink into it. The swoon was graceful and operatic, Lin being Lin. 'Seer,' she stuttered. 'Did you say Seer?'

Kate sat on the bed. 'Naff, right? Some new age rubbish. I'd put money that he drummed it into some impressionable kid and it spread from there.'

'Can I get a glass of water?' Lin batted her eyelashes and Kate snorted, it was the most contrived thing she had ever seen. Eric obliged, as he was already standing. 'Ms K sometimes you're just spooky. Young Miss Carol of the farm has just been filling my ears with the exact same effluent. Even she hasn't a clear idea who this Seer is, other than to be ass-puckeringly scared of him.'

'That's right—you found someone who lived at the farm?'

'She was there for a bit.' Lin poked her lip thoughtfully and too hard, as though it were numb. 'Odd getting her to talk. Like it'd been eating her. Eating her up for a long time.'

Kate looked to Eric who gave a little nod of confirmation, and don't think *that* escaped Lin's attention. 'We think the Seer's keeping people trapped in the town. Or keeping them out. Or both. Might be why we couldn't find the place.'

Lin shuddered, eyes fixed on their collection scattered like a yarrow forecasting. It did draw the look. Same as it drew the gorge right up your throat. The air of the cramped room seemed somehow gelid around that table, the oxygen sluggish to circulate. 'He definitely does not want folk setting up farms nearby. Ms K, if that really is a pretty from the Seer you'll want it out of here before we can talk.'

'Kill it with fire?'

'Oh my no.' Joking aside, the weird sheen to her eyes put the wind up Kate. Warning her jolly retriever might bite. 'If my working hypothesis is working, then fire won't do a damn thing against *him*. Not now.'

'What have you learned, Lin?' What dark hole have you stuck your head into?

'Take those outside. Then I'll spill.'

Eric retained his letter—that went nowhere without a fight. The rest they scooped into a bowl and tucked outside the door behind the trashcan. The air indoors immediately seemed cleaner, easier to breathe. Only now did Kate accept how she and Eric had been huddled sucking fear all day like exhaust. 'So how did you track down Carol?'

The prospect of showing off brought old Lin most of the way back. Hard to credit your reliance on that satisfied gleam of her smile. 'I *am* rather clever, you know.'

'We're vaguely aware of it.'

'This is the information age: nobody's further than a title search and quick trawl of their social media away. And man, you ought to see Carol Meyersen's feed: reads like it was written by the Babysitter Club, so of course my first thought was serial killer. Had to be. When I said I was investigating weird shit near her old farm she grudgingly nominated a café to meet. Nice to see someone with the smarts to not go inviting strangers into their home.'

Not specifically looking at Eric but he squirmed nonetheless. After all, she and Kate could have been maniacs wandering around at night like that, they could have been anything.

'I got there early and took a seat facing the door. Was keen to see if I could recognise Carol when she arrived.' No surprise there: Lin was a social piranha. She'd nibble you to bones with one look.

'I'd already figured a bit. She wouldn't be cutesy-poo—her profile was compensation. No nine-to-fiver either if she had leisure to meet in the middle of the day. My dollar was on Carol inhabiting a more marginal life. She'd have piercings, a trendy haircut. Probably a passing interest in slap 'n tickle on the side, you know, a bit of elbow grease … sorry, just messing with you Eric, don't bust an artery.'

Their third wishing himself away through the floor. Good skin to hide a blush.

'Wasn't a bad spot to blow a lazy afternoon. Not many places do their own shortbread anymore. Lunch hour had split and it was mostly new mums escaping their houses; iced coffee on every table, towering whipped cream that rubbed off on the ceiling.

'That sort of glowy, mumbling atmos you'd feel safe, right? That's how I knew when Miss Carol arrived. Hairs went right up and stuck holes through my collar. I actually snuck a glance to see if I could slip out via the loo but monster prams were crammed in any way they could fit, to flee I'd have to go bouncing across the top.

'Anyways, wasn't time. The frowny stoic she entered with went his own way and here came Carol, smiling with a melancholy mouth. I got my first clear look at her and slowly settled back in my chair. There was a woman who looked worn down in her bones.

'She was definitely leaking a nasty ... I guess you'd say "aura." Like she'd stepped in something that wouldn't wash, not even if you scrubbed bloody, and she knew it. *Come on*, that long face challenged, *hate me and get it over with*.

'Which didn't make sense! Aside from the scratched-in resignation she seemed a solid enough little lass. You could totally picture her as a super helpful librarian.

'Scraping some decency together I thanked her for her time, and seeing the opportunity for an easy open mentioned that her friend didn't seem to like me much. That made the sun come out. If only my nerves weren't trying to slink away. Amused, she twisted to meet grumpypants' glare where he was taking it hot and bitter across the room. 'Nick? He's my neighbour. In the history of forever Nick's not met anyone he trusted.'

"He's here—must do alright by you."

"Practicing his Dad skills. Always wanted kids, I reckon. Not babies; grown kids he can ply with nuggets of hard earned wisdom. Insisted on being here in case you were planning to stuff my ass in your trunk.'

"Feel free to inform Nick's nuggets that my trunk is consent only." Good old Nick for managing to see past the vibe Carol put out; at ground zero I was finding the other cheek hard to turn. Maybe it was like being colourblind.

'Cool as a cucumber Miss Carol orders herself a tea and I swear the next words out of her mouth were, 'Of course I've heard of the town. Who hasn't?"

'Who hasn't?' Kate pulled her hair, outraged. 'Try the utilities, council, government, everyone at our work, *us* until this week ..!'

'Ok, quit shooting the messenger.'

'The town's a ghost! *Nobody's* heard of it!'

'Well apparently it was something of a bugaboo when Carol grew up.'

'Well fuck her childhood, and the horse it rode in on, its mother, its mother's horses …'

Lin raised her eyebrows with exaggerated politeness. 'May I continue?'

'Oh I can't wait to hear more.'

'Ahem. When Carol was small, some wire and two cans radio spot got a prank call nobody ever figured out. Weirdest thing was the call wasn't a call. Didn't come in on any phone. The station picked it up as an intruding broadcast. Not that knowing the punchline would have improved it from the sounds of things.'

'Were *we* the punchline?'

'Kate! I *will* send you to your room!' That made them chuckle, looking around the tiny murky space.

'Carol was in the car with her mother at the time, and she said they ended up pulled to the verge to sit in the dust and flies, listening. Like nothing else could be going on, not while it was happening. All life had to stop.

'It was a young girl's voice. Young like Carol had been and her mother reached across and clasped her hand without ungluing her eyes from the dash. The girl on the radio was weeping. Ugly, hitching and gasps like when you lose control of yourself. A lot of crackle on the line with the signal fading, the complaining presenter poking through. What with his squawking you couldn't hear all of it, wanted to scream *shut up shut up!* and pummel the dash like he could hear you. And there was music, as though off in the distance. Old music that sawed up and down your nerves.

'The jumble made young Carol want to run away. The girl in the radio said *she'd* run off from home, her Daddy wouldn't let her pierce her ears. But now a bad man, a very bad man was keeping her in "the town" and she didn't know where she was. A Mrs Oxfort who was there with her said it was supposed to be nice but wasn't, only when Mrs Oxfort talked about it she always started scratching her long thin arms and then Mr Singh said shush or the Seer would hear.

'The bad man was always monitoring even when you couldn't see him, that's why they called him the Seer, he had *ways*. He could make *things* to watch you. And do other things.

'It was the kind of experience that hurts your insides. During that long wait glued to hot upholstery while the car ticked, listening to the other girl's misery drip from the radio. Hearing that reedy sobbing out of tinny speakers asking over and over for somebody to have her Mummy and Daddy come get her. Carol's mother's hand had clamped convulsively at that and Carol squirmed uncomfortably, wanting to be free.

'Her mother fussed over crushed fingers later. Wrapped peas from the freezer around Carol's purpling hand and gave her an icy pole for being a "good brave girl" and for not telling Daddy. Carol felt neither good nor brave but the correlation between action and reward had always been mysterious.

'For weeks after Carol was denied free run of the farm, but her parents were only human. A thousand everyday squabbles nibbled into vigilance until within a month she roamed as widely as ever. The girl on the radio became no more than a shadow.

'But that was not the story Carol came to the café to tell me. 'I thought you were here to ask about the Seer,' she says, wrinkles folding her forehead. The bad man.

"Well I am now, now I know he's got something to do with this town. What can you tell me?'

'And Carol hardens abruptly, looks ready to punch her teacup through the table. I tell you, do not mess with librarians. She snarled, 'That fucker took my dog.''

Time had been a smeary concept to young Carol. The boon was only appreciated as a harried adult looking back. From frequent dispersal to chores even her family blurred in mind's eye, only sharp when they stood in front of her demanding something. An introspective child, used to her own company she was sensitive to how immensely she did not understand what was going on. Most of the time her feelings were panicky and adrift, the world rubbed in her face.

It seemed they had always rattled about lonely rural properties. Places where bugs with questing antennae tapped their way in, dust slithered out, and the weather blew indifferent to walls raised against it. In recounting what happened to Lin so many years later the dreaminess of her childhood coloured everything.

The only two genuine anchors of Carol's youth had been temperature; that flipping coin of stifling or shivering; and Max. Good old Max.

Ostensibly a working kelpie, Max had proven so useless his owner hadn't even considered the dignity of a stroll to the back paddock. Just a chunk of brick and a ditch for Max. Threw some beer bottles after, belched to relieve their conscience, and drove away. These days folk'd get their asses fined to the devil or jailed for such callousness, *if* they got caught.

Carol's father had spotted two pale eyes peering from the ditch, that eerie kelpie stare that slices steel, and almost spun off the road thinking it was a ghost. Wouldn't that be something: obliterating his entire young family because of an outback spook.

Nobody screamed. Carol was too surprised, the front seats had obscured her view of the oncoming accident. Her mother alone managed a sort of agonised *mmph* with both hands pressed to her mouth as the car skidded to a rocking stop on its creaky shocks, and by then it was all over.

'Stay in the car!' Carol's father shouted, not meaning to shout, provoking his wife into thinking there was danger after all. He clambered from the car, a vulnerable figure all alone out there. *Now* Carol thought with a shiver without knowing what it meant. *Now it will come for him.* Her chest too tight for speaking, she frantically willed her Daddy to get back in the car.

What he did was walk a ways to the ditch and then stand staring into it for an awful long time. Carol slithered across the seat to press against the chipped window and thought her father's broad shoulders collapsed, he collapsed. Must have been a lie of the cruddy glass because he returned to the car with his normal resolute step. A mind made up, always sure of what he would do. A cornerstone. Ignoring their shrill queries he opened the back.

Carol's father approached the ditch again, slowly, with a spread picnic rug from the boot. And the snarl of hair he retrieved never barked or shrieked. Not even when, bundled up, the rescuee was laid across the back seat.

Carol got shifted up front to sit on her mother's knee. Technically against the road rules which she was very clear on, especially those about seatbelts, but they did not know this animal. You can't trust a sick scared dog, her mother whispered, to be anything but sick and scared.

Carol squirmed around to meet those remarkable pale

eyes watching her steadily from the cowl of the rug. Hard to recognise a dog in that half crushed face. *She* could tell he was a good boy and murmured it, 'Good boy, good boy,' to help him be brave as the car bumped along and hurt his dented head.

Later that night after she was supposed to have been tucked in, Carol lingered in the dark hallway with frankfurts of ice for toes. She was listening to her parents as they sat round the table with cups of tea, two from the same teabag. *Eavesdropping*, her teacher said, *was a nasty habit* but how else was she supposed to find anything out? A touch of information could assuage the gnawing anxiety—although it frequently made it worse.

The vet bill had been staggering. China clattered. After a long silence Carol's father hoarsely confessed that he regretted stopping the car, a bit. Her mother held his hand.

Hearing that, a tiny part inside the shivering girl hardened into dead volcanic stone. Even in such a miniscule way, she had not known it was possible to hate her parents.

Which was how Max came home to them. Rescued into a mucky stinky family dog. He was Carol's responsibility, insofar as messing up wouldn't hurt the hip pocket further. Seeing as the girl could hardly get a spoon of breakfast until Max had had his there were limits to how wrong she could get it.

Such had been the conclusion of the moment. In retelling, adult Carol had to wonder if the world, struggling to make ends meet, simply had no time. She'd been left to her own narrow conclusions as to why. Things at the farm had not been going well. Even sheltered from the brunt Carol and Max could not help being aware. Both were smart enough to stay out of the way.

Driven from the house, Carol spent her mornings bounding through paddocks while Max cruised low in the scratchy grass like a land shark, circling, and she'd laugh 'cause he couldn't herd her. Everybody knew Max couldn't herd *anything*.

The grass was perfect for it: tall, ravenous, lashing her limbs in a stinging hatchwork that would heal overnight so she could do it all again. Winter, spring and summer grey rain had pelted down and even now the ground wobbled underfoot. Like racing across a buried mattress.

Splots in her peripheral vision. They surrounded Carol before she realised and joy flagging she stumbled to a halt. Only unsure as yet, but plenty more emotions flickering on the horizon. Small weird things in the grass. She bent to look.

Dark violet almost to black, curved, hard and hornlike. They looked like leeches, dark leeches stretching out of the waving seed heads on every side.

Even as her small chest hitched in to scream Carol managed to choke it off; she'd heard again and again how her parents weren't raising a squealing ninny. The "leeches" weren't squirming eagerly toward her pulse. That's all you were to a leech: a big sack of blood.

She touched one lightly with a wondering finger. It was like a purple-black piece of stone. No threat then, surely no threat. And it wasn't like she was on her own, here came Max pushing his way through to bump her knee with a wet nose. No reason not to keep on.

Five uncertain paces on Carol found *actual* stones. Old shattered rocks had been stacked in a tall pile at the far end of the paddock. Tall like a grownup, taller than her. Of a white glinty stone she knew she'd not seen around here.

Carol could not conceive of any reason for her parents to build such a thing. So perhaps it was here before they came, and she'd somehow missed it until now? The grass *had* been growing like crazy. The grass could conceal a lot of things.

She circled it. With its heavy base sunk into the oozing muck the rock pile looked like it had been there always. Before the paddock. Before the fences or the farm. No chance of investigating the mystery any closer: the rocks looked … nasty. Like all the spiders and bugs of the world were quivering inside, just waiting to spill out, a shuddering tide of bugs.

Ssh, Carol. Close your eyes, breathe deep. One two three four five, five fingers, until she wasn't going to shriek anymore and could open. A time out, how mother showed her, where the world got pushed away for a few precious breaths. The antidote to stop from hitting anyone—especially, heaven forbid, her teacher. Seeing her parents' disappointment again might kill her.

It wasn't like Carol was nuts; Max didn't like the rocks either. The muscular dog shouldered her back and barked and barked with his peculiar crushed voice, somewhere between creak and groan, a broken toy being squeezed. He was all bristled up like a lion. Had there been a throat instead of mouldy old rocks he'd have torn it out.

That more than anything sent Carol flying back the way she'd come. Her mother's voice, tense with worry, *Can't trust a sick scared dog.* No matter how much you love them.

However she was bursting with it, Carol had no opportunity to tell what she'd seen. Ugly shouting reached her long before she reached home and her gut settled on dread.

Their neighbour, if properties so distant could still be called that, had hitched a trailer to his decrepit museum piece tractor and driven over with a couple of his cows. Arriving, he'd shoved them into the front yard where the argument exploded.

The vehicle's huge tyres were gouged right into Carol's mother's flowerbeds. Carol's mother herself stood with thin hands clenched in her hair to physically contain her upset. The frail raggedy flowers were the only thing solely *hers*, a modest indulgence outside her role of selfless mother and wife. A reminder of who she'd once been: a young student who'd loved flowers in a jar to brighten her dorm. Now trampled and torn up.

Somewhere in the stratosphere above Carol's head the adults went on yelling. The unintelligible storm might as well be on another planet. She was transfixed by the neighbour's cows. The cows were not right.

Out of all the stock on a farm she had always liked cows. Inquisitive beasts despite the decades of meat-or-milk indignity. Cows tended to try to work out what you were doing. And so quiet! Walk to a fence line, turn, and twenty of the big soft-snorting beasts would be right behind like in a children's game. Purple tongues slithering at their nostrils as they tried to puzzle you out.

Every year her parents locked up the house while they went to protest live export, "torture ships" they called them. Carol had never been allowed to examine the stacks of flyers: Dad said the conditions the big gentle animals were crammed into (let alone the unregulated horror at the end) would give her nightmares.

The first thing Carol noticed on these huddled, not quite grown cows were their big square heads. Twisted stiffly up and to the side like their beautiful muscular necks were cramped. Spasms ran along their skin in seismic waves. Frothy drool splattered to the ground beneath, drowned her mother's trampled flowers.

Off the trailer they stumbled to a halt with hinds drooping out of step from the forelimbs, trembling and unwilling to budge further. Like they were being forced to walk on fire. Biting her lip uncertainly, Carol had to peer closer to realise why. Her stomach immediately began hiccupping in loops and swirls.

Socks, her mind stammered. On all four feet it looked like the straining, flinching cows were wearing terrible socks. A clear line around each ankle as though drawn by charcoal stick with healthy leg above and suppurating sores below, where flies vibrated with repulsive greed. And the "socks" were falling down, falling down, falling down, that furred skin hanging too loose.

As she watched with cringing horror a swathe of skin just peeled away. Beneath the shouting she shouldn't have heard the grotesque sucking sound but she did. The sock slipped off and flopped into the dust leaving mottled red and black lumps exposed. The flies rejoiced. The cow groaned.

Carol would not allow herself to see any more. That was the only control she exercised over her life. As disregarded by the screaming adults as ever, she dashed to the house and slipped indoors. Managed to get all the way to her room and softly softly close the door, shutting it all out before convulsively vomiting on the rug.

The tears she'd first begun choking back in the paddock forced their way out, her small body trying to expel the wretchedness she'd been witness to. And her mother was not there to put a cool washcloth on her forehead, nobody to stroke her hair and tell her it would be ok.

Adult Carol shook her head. The memory had an unpleasant taste that tea only partly covered. 'It's weird to think so now, but back at the start there'd been wonder along with the fear, to be discovering such strange things. Kids don't know a damn thing about anything.'

'Of course as adults we're so much wiser.' Just to get that smile again. Carol obliged wanly.

'Well at least we can find shit out. I'd hardly go calling myself a scholar but you know after something crazy happens how later you try to understand, apply some kind of framework? Even if it doesn't make sense you try because hey, what else— just accept the universe is crazy?'

Lin snorted. 'I've got a friend who does just that.'

'Not me. I could never shake it all out of my head and eventually it occurred to read up a little. Have you ever heard of holy fire?'

Lin had not. Religion had not distinguished itself, offering her little grace and much snide condemnation; being holier than thou required a thou to spit on.

Carol sipped her tea. 'That's ok, it was a bit rhetorical. Holy fire is a sickness you get from eating contaminated grain. Mainly rye which was, like, poor people's bread. In fact in ye olde times people thought lumpy was how grain was supposed to look, called it cockspurs, didn't even know it was an infection. That's how widespread it was.'

'Gross.' The baking smells were no longer so enticing.

'Gross is right. Very tiny amounts can be used to induce birth, but an uncontrolled dose messes bloodflow to bits furthest from your heart: fingers and toes. Hot fiery pain. Messes up your brain real bad, brings on gangrene, even. People, livestock. Doesn't sound very holy, huh?'

Lin was seeing it—psychosomatic pins prickled her extremities. 'Mostly poor people. So of course they were being punished by God.'

'You got it. Holy fire burned in fierce epidemics following wet seasons. They needed to believe something was responsible, that there was something they could do. Apply a framework.'

'Blame somebody.' It was what folk were good at.

'It's not like everyone was just being an asshole rabbiting on about divine wrath.'

Lin crossed her arms. 'Go on then. Shock me.'

'I forget the exact date but there was this dude, De la Valloire, who must have been wicked rich because he set up a hospital specifically to treat holy fire. Dedicated it to Saint Anthony, and it was such a great idea that a whole order of monks springboarded off it—holy fire became St Anthony's Fire. They had to paint the hospitals stark glaring red so the half crazed peasants staggering up the road on their rotting feet would know where to go. How brave's that, huh?'

'Painting a barn?'

Carol made a face at her. 'Signing up to fight something they scarcely understood. Must have been knee deep in despair at times over the sheer mystery and horror of the task, but they stepped up anyways.'

The café was not a good place to be telling such a story, even in a private voice. The herd of mothers surrounding them, each at her own table, could push the influence off because refusing to dwell on bad news was how adults got on with their day.

But the infants were raw, without defences. The prams were shaking. They began to fuss and cry like bobby calves.

From that point on young Carol's life became increasingly bounded by things that were not normal. Previously she'd been permitted to undertake the long walk to the postbox and back alone. It was one of her big-girl chores. She liked to handle the smooth white envelopes, they seemed important, even when she was a tad late and they came out marred by the coiled munching of hungry slugs and snails.

And it wasn't *really* dangerous. If the plume of dust wasn't enough of a giveaway you could hear cars kilometres off. But now her father had to accompany her, tossing the task right back to little kid territory. Which also meant post got put off to whenever he was available, instead of when the urge struck Carol to rush outside and tramp the weedy verge into fresh air and silence, where moth riddled leaf chandeliers sieved the light and tapped her head like old friends reminding her *you love this*.

Instead, here went her father. Slouching in front with hands in pockets and eyes as empty as a phone call, not even trying to make it fun. Max took rear guard, which left Carol piggy in the middle.

The convoy was why she didn't immediately understand when her father held his hand out behind and she crashed into it. 'Stay there honey. Just … stay there.' His voice sounded strained but that was nothing new.

'Stay Max,' she hissed rebelliously. The obedient kelpie crouched, his pale eyes bright. It was his new habit to crowd close enough to trip over but Carol did not mind—not when she woke to the congested rasp from her closet of somebody breathing through their mouth in the dark. Or when she peered across a paddock trying to decide if that was a figure staring at her from the other side. Anyone who wanted Carol would have to come through Max first.

Her father was kicking around, picking up a stick because mud was caked around the outside of their postbox. Not a little bit either.

A cluster of boxes huddled like gossips alongside the meeting with the main road; the postman could hardly be asked to slog down all those meandering driveways, roads in their own right. His next shift would be up before he'd even returned from deep in the fields.

It was a bit of local colour that some neighbours got elaborate about their postboxes, repurposing old milk canisters or other bits of interesting equipment; repainting every spring in proud pig pink or cow spots. Carol averted her eyes from the latter. She did not like cows anymore.

By contrast their postbox was just a basic tin box on a post. No need for a lock, her mother said with forced cheer, any thief who wanted their bills was welcome to them. But theirs was the only one smeared.

Using the stick with his other sleeve pressed to his nose her father flipped it open and oh no. That was not mud caked on the outside and packed solid within.

The smell Carol knew too well from clearing Max's logs off the lawn, only this was worse. A rotting stench from the hindquarters of something mostly dead that did not know it yet, that still strained at the processes of life, pretending all was normal.

And … was that a slime of ..? Dark, foamy and organic, oozing out. Crushed tomatoes in a bowl, or that texta she split staining the rug and her hands so her mother screamed thinking her scalded and wept with relief when she trod in the rest of the mess, kissing her daughter all over and Carol sick with not knowing what she'd done now.

Her father dropped his stick and gagged once, a harsh *gak* not unlike those Max made from his broken head. And then he was herding Carol back. Doing his best to block with his body what she had already seen. 'Come on, back to the house.'

'But Dad it's …'

'Pronto young lady!' It was not so much his hysteria that got her going as the expression which had become familiar these days: fixed, blank. Her father's mind was away to something more critical, and would not be lured back by shouts or demands.

She backed up but a great surge of anger at her powerlessness swept over Carol, clenching her small fists. She would wait.

Waiting was an old friend. Perhaps tonight she could overhear them discussing it in their hushed indoors voices and learn something that way.

However, following dinner her parents went to bed without talking or so much as looking at each other, let alone Carol. She brushed her teeth extra hard until they hurt and took her frustrations to sleep.

That night there was a loud crash from the front loungeroom. A yelp of distress from her father who charged to investigate and in bare feet ran over the shards of window scattered all through the carpet. There was that colour again—the scalded shade that made Carol's head ache.

She held Max safely back in the hallway, although now her mother turned the light on and everyone could see the terrible mess, and what had been flung through the front window. A severed cow's foot. Only not severed. The ends were raggedy, *stringy*. It had rotted off.

'Yeah well fuck you too!' Carol's mother bellowed angrily out into the night.

'Honey, just … help me here, would you?'

In slippers she helped her husband limp to safety. Pinching glass out with tweezers required iron nerves, but she was so enraged with nowhere to go that she trembled and fizzed just like those cows had done.

Carol twisted that thought off right there. Moths and buzzing things were already making their way in the newly broken aperture to investigate the orange-lit loungeroom, and she silently withdrew before her parents noticed.

Wasn't hard to guess what they believed: that the neighbours were to blame, but Carol had never heard the gravel crunch of a car pulling away. The bad person responsible had never left. Was lurking, breathing rapidly in her closet at night, and now finally she remembered the radio broadcast. The bad man.

Under his influence the cheerful façade collapsed. Her parents became snappy at the slightest infraction, and Carol was no longer allowed to flee outside. Never knew what she'd do wrong next. Probably nothing. Nobody was sleeping, and indoors you had the constant sense of someone behind you—that a stranger was in the house. Even in the room.

Carol had seen her parents sneaking along the hallway pressed to the wall like cartoon characters. They bared their teeth and yanked open doors as though hoping to surprise somebody, then stared numbly into the revealed space, already unsure what they'd only been vaguely aware of looking for. It wasn't Carol—if they saw her, they yelled.

One night when Carol when to wash for bed her toothbrush was burned. Slumped and melted into its water glass, although nothing else on the sink seemed touched by heat. Not knowing what to do she carried the glass to her mother, her only reward some muttering about dodgy wiring.

It wasn't that a toothbrush cost so much, even with so little to go around. It was the trip into town. The way they had to shun other people's eyes, hurry instead of stopping to admire things they way they used to in the lazy afternoon sun, giggling and pointing them out in fake posh voices. Not enough petrol this month to make the long drive into next town, which was their new, twice as expensive way to get groceries.

Misery made all faces long, although if her parents' things were also brutalised they were not letting on. Carol found Bronto her stuffed brontosaurus crammed headfirst into a crack in the wall that opened up as the foundations sank and nobody had yet plastered over. Pulling him out proved a mistake. He was gummed with filth.

Again she brought the evidence to her parents with a hopeful face. *Fix this, can't you? This is your job. You fix everything.* Before the stain even started rinsing out Bronto's seams began giving way from so many trips through the washer. It left his face mottled, an unwholesome fungal grey that seemed to be staring at her in the dark so Carol put him on the porch and the next day her father threw him out.

Dad was slow moving, slow reacting, fatalistic. Both her parents were beginning to accept everything as the new normal—or at least unavoidable, which was the next best. That was the scariest part. Something bad wanted them driven off and her parents who should have been coping and organising and planning just ... stood there. Hollowed out, hardly her parents at all. Just hard upright shells like the cicadas left clinging to the trees.

And so the core was scooped out of young Carol's existence. This other influence creeping close to fill it up.

One more thing happened before they finally left, before those months spent sleeping in the car while they searched for a new home. Max was barking. That was what woke Carol and why she went into the front room. Max was a good boy, he never barked in the house.

In the dark she felt her way with her toes. The boarded up front room window let in a steady stream of cold and more insects than usual. Especially at night, when they felt bolder.

'*Max,*' Carol whisper-hissed, not wanting her parents to wake up. '*Max! Shh!*' If she could get him back to her room everything would be fine. It was her job to protect Max as much as he her. She squinted.

The figure slithering about the shadows of the front room was too upright to be Max. Max was no longer anywhere, Max was gone. And her father knelt helplessly beside holding his hands out to it, turning a bloodless face toward Carol as she entered.

Carol's mother was barking in Max's broken voice. Sharp and loud in the confined space, barking and barking. The spray from her mouth was only red as it hit the wall.

'Are you *happy* about this?'

Kate was excited, practically bouncing around the room. Lin's mere presence had revived her, suggesting the possibility of action. 'Carol's dog crossed over. Subjects vanished from the institute. What have they got in common?'

'They make me want to poop my pants?'

'All prefigured by the Seer's rock piles, his sentinels or whatever they are, and other stuff popping up. Are you with me yet?'

Two shrugs. 'Can't say we are.'

'The figurine in my handbag, *that's* how I was able to reach through and snag Ben's letter.'

'Your creepy little finger-doll.'

'Ok look we are calling it literally anything else."

'Digit Debbie?'

'No.'

'Baby's First Manicure.'

'Your ability to make suggestions goes in time out, starting now. These things aren't just eyes for the Seer or—or contaminants to make your life go tits-up. They make you more likely to, I don't know, touch the town.'

'Ah yes that makes sense why it's a finger.'

'Oh my god no that's not why. I think their effect might be cumulative, the longer you hold it, the stronger the effect. I think this Seer's inadvertently handed us a key.'

'Handed us a key.'

Eric shushed Lin. 'Why is that good?'

Kate's eyes gleamed. 'We're going to take what he's given us out to the vacant site and use it to access the town.'

CHAPTER EIGHT

RADIANT

It was supposed to be cooler moving around at night. Not to mention less exposed. Those were the platitudes of their hurried planning in a room wrapped tight in fusty motel curtains.

Instead the anonymity of the city had felt safer, and the hot air shut like an industrial press. Through the smeared, claustrophobic windscreen a yellow oval of broken track jostled and jounced. Dizzy with headache they soaked through their clothes in seconds.

Kate risked a hand off the wheel to rummage the tangle of crackling plastic stuffed down the centre console. 'Lin, you didn't take *all* the painkillers?'

'It was a long drive, ok! Felt sick.' Childlike and malingering. Even that was a relief: they'd been enduring *this is where I die* in white-knuckled silence around every bend for an hour now, the vegetation rushing by like a tunnel. Kate fretted over the headlights, but driving without had proven the kind of idiocy only a tourist would dream up.

'It's different.' Silence. More jostling, a squeak from the suspension that made you want to tear your hair out. 'I *said* it looks *different*, Ms K. Are you even listening?'

'I hear you. What do you want—it's dark!'

Lit horribly by the dash with her bones poking through, Lin made the sort of noise that gets you kicked out of class. 'So you're positive we're going the right way.'

'Oh yep. One hundred percent.' There was no way to be sure.

Their bustling lives had revolved around where you sprang from, were headed, and the all important *why*. An embedding that was just not possible out here in this rushing vortex of leaves. Turning flat waxy surfaces to bounce the high beams— like eyes, they were. A thousand eyes every side that opened and shut in the dark.

Being responsible for dragging the gang along Kate wasn't about to confess the map had dissolved into a blizzard of crumbs when she tried to pull it from her pocket. Elucidation would hardly bring happiness; really she was doing them a favour.

Twigs squealed on the paintwork and Kate grimaced and strangled the wheel. Lin at least ought to be more up for this. It was right up her alley: Lin's Big Midnight Adventure! Not huddled in the passenger seat, cranky and shivering in the humidity. All Lin was about tonight was pinching her sodden clothes away from her skin.

Maybe the lack of talisman was bringing her down. Eric, hunched awkwardly in the back and yet to say boo had his brother's letter. Kate's handbag harboured a creepy ass dollie. Lin got ..? Perhaps she was not telling yet. She always did like to feel special.

Oh. 'Oh.' Damn. She'd said it out loud.

Ghost-lit Lin jerked upright, anxiety yanking her strings. 'Oh? Oh what? What now?'

'Why are we stopping?' the back seat chorus chimed in.

They *were* on the right track, as broken and beat up as it appeared by night. One that rolled them to a stop in front of the big old lunatic gate in the middle of nowhere. Tortured metal bars crisscrossed darkness, and Orphan Annie's headlights failed to probe any deeper.

Kate had genuinely forgotten the barrier, or more likely pushed it from mind. Didn't she have enough to worry about? She rolled down her window and the cicadas and other night insects hissed mockingly, as though daring them to exit their little tin can.

'Where's the other one?' Pawing feebly at her seatbelt Lin sampled the test pattern of panic. An octave higher and she'd rival the bugs, who already seemed to want to drill through their heads.

Previously the gate had been propped like a souse between two pillars of shoddily stacked white stone, bleached turds crapped out by some vast prehistoric beast. Now the iron poles it attached to were bare, so narrow it appeared to float in mid-air.

One of the rock piles now stood inexplicably in the middle of the path, blocking their way. Kate cranked the glass back up, having confirmed nothing except that she had to be out of her mind.

'The other what?' Through a haze of motion sickness Eric was catching on that something had gone terribly askew. Kate glanced in the rear vision mirror but without light the cramped rear seat was difficult to see, Eric nothing more than a lump of complaining shadow.

She drummed her hands restlessly on the wheel. Lin had a point. *Where was the other one?* 'Well. I say we can't sit here all night with our thumbs up our backsides.'

'How have you even been steering with your—don't. Kate, seriously, don't. *This car is rented!*'

She nearly stalled it like an asshole, the shoebox engine doing its mighty best to roar. All three heads knocked back with a coconut "clunk!" that hardly boded well for the brains inside. The out of control jolt of a rollercoaster over the edge, nothing you could do, the future out of your hands. Terrifying. Liberating.

Kate's foot was locked, tromping the accelerator with all her might as they rushed forward. You would have to break her fingers to prise the wheel free. Every moment she had sat in a car, from presumed child to adult, she'd been waiting for an accident—now, no longer passive, it was finally here. The crash!

The bonnet lurched drunkenly toward unseen stars, mounting rocks. The scraping groan through the undercarriage was horrendous. Kate was sure they would be hung up and trapped.

Her eyes bone dry from not wanting to miss a second: *that's it oh hell I've killed everybody*. In a saner moment she might have chided herself for being a terrible person.

The rock sentinel burst apart beneath their assault. A flood of soured fluid slapped across the windscreen, coughed from a plague victim. Orphan Annie flopping back down, wheels digging in and occupants rattled like dice in a cup.

Clawing toward another gear Kate hammered at the wiper control to clear the glass before they impaled themselves on a tree. Too many things happening to keep up.

Before she was ready, second impact. The gate clanged wide as she'd known it would, having seen the shitty fastenings firsthand.

By the time the bars completed their violent arc and came shuddering back they were already speeding through and the gate rang off the bumper.

'Ha!' Kate was unable to contain herself.

Fishtailing wildly, she risked a peek in the rear view to ensure all parties made it safely—Eric's perch was in greatest danger of getting bounced through the roof, if not sliced in half by his seatbelt. As much as attention was needed elsewhere Kate's bloodshot eyes locked onto that sliver of reflection.

She struggled to decipher what was back there. Understanding short circuited under the load while a mineral stink billowed out to fill the cab. It was like the vehicle fractured around her. The only remaining sound was air hissing out as though she were a kettle.

Rocks, picked out in flashes by the jerking light. Ancient, pale and *looming*. Scraping the car's ceiling, the sides, impossibly big. More sensed as threat than seen, like a great wave ready to crash down.

Did it progress beyond the physical boundaries of the car, through the walls? Her brain got traction by paring understanding down to the bits it could manage. The back seat was filled with the gate's second sentinel, heaped where Eric should be. Only now did it come through how Annie groaned under the load, rear axel practically digging a trench.

'Kate? Kate, watch the road. What are you *doing*?' Lin twisted in listless slow motion and saw for herself. She proved a natural screamer and hammered the back of Kate's headrest, 'Stop! Stop!' Kate could not get her breath, or think. She could obey. 'Stop!'

Her face a tight mix of rage and fear Lin was already hauling her seat forward for access to the back. '*CAN'T HAVE THIS ONE!*' she bellowed and was blinding to look at. As soon as her hands touched them the rocks began to shudder and split apart. The smell intensified.

Within its chrysalis an insect dissolves down to sludge, released from that terrible burden of self—but a person will never be a bug. It was Eric's fingers, untransformed, that poked through the slit to clutch and stab frantically at the air. He was waking into a nightmare.

A moment ago he had been enclosed, with no sense of self or how he got there. Peacefully erased. Knotted upon himself like a small thing dropped into somebody's pocket.

Until he heard far-off strains of music that seemed to drift closer. What was that? What was it? Curiosity and longing were at the heart of Eric's quest for his brother, and could not be removed without undoing him utterly. Curiosity was a state of existence, anathema to the blank peace that wrapped him.

His prison expressed its displeasure immediately. It grew hotter, and Eric was squeezed, struggling in a giant fist. He heard his bones creak, about to split and rend the fleshy stuff within into shards. And then Lin seized both of his wrists and pulled.

Kate's wits only engaged as Lin was dragging the curly haired man free. In the feeble glow of the dome light she rushed around to help.

Eric was wailing in the high frantic register of a squashed animal as he was hauled out of the car. Lanky arms and legs shooting in all directions—she expected him to fly into pieces like the map. Another gush of that foetid fluid followed, slopping onto the ground.

Kate had to take over holding him secure to the burned earth as Lin slumped off to one side, coughing in great tearing heaves like sheets of lung stripping free. Retrieving Eric seemed to have been her last hurrah. Lin's beautiful long hair shrouded her face and caught flecks of spit, fish in a net.

'Eric? Eric?' Rapidly sifting her useless first aid catechisms Kate was not so much calling as checking it was really him. But on Eric her brittle voice acted like a balm, confirming his identity. His limbs settled like fallen leaves. Sobs began squeezing their way out.

Well … ok then. Kate sat back. She recognised the importance of a release valve: the stiff-upper types too stubborn to cry it out tended to spike massive coronaries before forty. She waited, on the edge of a puddle of light that did not go far, the milky liquid congealing in the charcoal around her feet, and felt a wave of euphoria. They'd done it. They'd beaten what the Seer had to throw at them.

After a bit Eric wiped his face matter of factly. He struggled to sit, keen to confirm with his own eyes the confines of the car were *over there* while he was *here*, no longer trapped. His other senses could not be trusted. 'Did you hear that?' he croaked.

Kate winced uneasily. 'I heard Lin breaking the scream barrier in my ear.'

'Music. I heard music. Old … old music.'

'What, in the rocks? You heard music in the rocks?'

'Think I was closer. To the town. Think … I was s'posed to come out there, not back here. Something went wrong. Don't know why I'm here again.'

'Don't say you're *annoyed* Lin pulled you out?'

He shrugged, either not knowing or not wanting the ungrateful possibility confirmed. 'Couldn't get through.' He'd been so close. 'Might've been squashed in there forever.' Who was to say the bastard rock piles hadn't slurped up other seekers, digested them slowly?

Not yet altogether Eric bit at his thumbnail, muttering, *'Don't know why I'm here again,'* until with a grimace he seemed to notice the fluid he was slick with.

With shaky hands he began dumping flat water over himself from the canteen, shaking it out to the last drop. Kate was instantly vile with envy. Heat baked like sickness out of every surface, especially the charcoal they sat in. Felt like her brain was coddling in her head. 'We might have needed that water, you know.'

He stripped moisture from his arms with quick efficient movements. 'It's not good. Not good to touch the rocks.'

'What, your skin'll fall off or something?' Belatedly recalling Carol's trembling drooling cows Kate regretted the levity.

The reek had settled into the car, made itself at home. Kate was never going to see her deposit on Orphan Annie again. Fortunately Eric was a man prepared, if not of action: he still had the metal tongs clanging from his belt. Handy for removing the collapsed pile of rocks from the back seat. He and Kate worked in bursts, chucking lumps over their shoulder to clatter on the road before ducking out to gulp at the insect laden air. Making sure none of the others were looking Kate slipped one of the least disgusting chunks into her handbag: a rock slightly bigger than her fist, veined with what looked like quartz.

Once they had finished there were more problems: Eric and Lin in no way wanted to abandon Annie to walk into the dark. Luckily, anticipating insurrection Kate had already pocketed the keys. Besides, with lights and engine off it felt less of a refuge.

Lin rolling her torch in her hands, sulky and fractious. Do not drop that light like the last one young lady, you won't get another. Eric straining with nervous energy, *so close, so close.* His scare seemed to have stuck a pin in him.

And Kate? She felt vague and disconnected. Irritated with her companions and on the verge of sweeping them behind her. She ought to resist if she was to continue playing well with others.

Eric flitted to her shoulder; incumbent then on Lin to drag herself along or be left behind. 'So how does this work?'

'We walk to …' Kate broke off with a sardonic laugh. 'I don't know why I'm saying that. Honestly? We're off the rails, experimenting. Isn't that exciting?' That ought to have got a rise from Lin's rigid corpse, but no joy. All they got were her listless footfalls crunching behind.

Kate sniffed and cracked open her handbag to stir the broken pieces of dollie, the shrivelled finger in its twist of cheap motel toilet paper. The nail had already slit through and scratched her unpleasantly.

Otherwise the pieces lay passive, although she got a strong impression they'd have liked to stir the shards of her had circumstance shaken out differently. 'Keep a hold on your brother's letter, and let's see what we can see.'

Not good enough for Eric. Swivelling his head with little jerky motions. 'Is that a record player?'

All Kate heard was a too loud crunch from behind, and swung around. 'What now?'

What now? Lin now. An indistinct lump face down on the ground where ants and spiders and God knows what else could get her.

At first Kate assumed she had tripped and smothered the urge to titter but her torch caught the tall woman's fingers out in front scratching weakly at the ground. *Scritch scratch.* Not trying to lever her up. The sight poured millipedes into Kate's belly.

What the hell? She shook off paralysis and jogged back, crouching to take hold of one of Lin's scratching hands. Had to overcome a hesitation to touch, unsure why the prospect made her skin crawl.

That hand was like a chunk of stone from Antarctica's heart. Kate pressed it briefly to her own overheated forehead, but put it away just as quick. This close a bad whiff was rising from Lin, like a family of mice caught in a heater. *I ought to have paid more attention! I thought she was just complaining.*

'Put out that light!' Lin snarled. No way was Kate about to do that out here, but she directed it carefully off to one side.

A smashed worm, Lin rocked herself into foetal position and a muffled gasp crept out. 'I think there's something wrong with me.' The admission let into the world to become really real, so huge and awful.

'Oh Lin. Did you eat something bad? I hope it was the pot noodles.'

'Hardly.' Lin uncurled a bit, snivelled. Kate brushed some charcoal from her face. 'More like something bit *me*. I went to Carol's farm.'

'*Why?* And you're only telling me this now?'

'Well excuse me all to hell for wanting to think things through. I made her take me. I wanted to see for myself.'

'Right. You mean you thought her story smelled of bullshit.'

'I wanted to *know*. This is like, like explorers used to face, Mawson with his feet peeling away and all. That's what we're doing too, isn't it? Going somewhere extraordinary?'

'That's the theory.'

'I'm sorry I didn't believe you from the start, Ms K.' She coughed. 'Don't know what I was expecting to find on a farm, anyhow. It's hardly like I could tell the difference between a backhoe and a regular ol' hoe.'

Kate stood, brushing off her hands. 'That's it. I'm leaving you to die.'

Lin's pained chuckle was almost lost as Eric hollered up

ahead. 'For Chrissake Eric!' Kate bellowed back. 'Would you wait! You don't even have a torch!'

'Don't let him get away, then. Help me up.'

'Adventure. Bloody idiot's going to trip and break his neck, that's where he's going.'

The truth had been Lin was not yet done with Carol's melancholy company.

Lin loved hearing about upbringings unlike her own and imagining herself there, variations that seemed as wild to her as landing on Mars. And young Carol seemed pretty switched on considering what she claimed to have been through.

Last but not least, she was in no way inclined to being told what to feel: not by authority, peers, and especially not some bullshit mystery repellent.

A few awkward u-turns at the start, but Miss Carol recalled the route better the further they drove. Perfectly fine with getting in a car with a stranger, too, and while the girl was doing her a solid Lin still scowled ferociously until Carol protested, 'What?'

'Nothing. It's nothing.' How much could even be left of her old digs after the harsh weather had been at it season after season?

Perhaps the navigation feat was less impressive seeing as there was nine-tenths of fuck-all out here. Just one lane looping drunkenly through scrub that split occasionally to one side or the other, revealing paddocks before swallowing them again.

Little dirt tracks snaked off the main tarmac, estuaries bristling with FOR SALE signs sagging from their stakes. Ring that number and nobody would pick up, most of the estate agencies having gone under themselves by now.

Where Carol timidly indicated the turnoff most of the postboxes had fallen down. Lin pulled over for a looki-loo, because something was wrong with her brain, wanting to see that.

She was not about to get a lot of help. Carol stayed glued to her seat, pouting falsely to cover unease and claiming she could hardly be expected to remember hers after all this time.

Lin was not fooled: at the *clunk* of the car door her own hackles had spiked. Temptation was high to just drive away but she started this. Owed herself a closer look.

Squinting across the empty road she wished vainly for a hat. The hot sun was turning her black hair into a curtain of fire. She kicked at the remains of one old box sunk in the grass, the rust had been ferocious. The fossilised black lumps inside preserved its original shape, but really, they could have been anything. Lin hoped they were anything.

Mulling it over, she returned to the car. Carol sat like a stone on the next seat while she deliberated. This was second thoughts territory, especially if Kate were here, whose mind scurried into all the dark nooks. But Lin was such a straight arrow. And imagining Kate's huffy disapproval sparked a warming glow. She turned the key and drove on.

Carol's rather dilapidated farmhouse still stood. They parked on the circular drive, a fancy touch that was probably more about manoeuvring tractors on and off the property. Carol and Lin disembarked, and stared at each other over Orphan Annie's nose.

Carol stirred uneasily. 'It's just like it was.' She sounded bewildered. 'I don't think anyone can have been out here since we left. Hardly anything's changed.'

'It's like the damn thing's been waiting for you or something. Talk about forgotten places! I ought to bring my mate Kate out here, her head would explode.'

'I never forgot. Not ever.' Carol rubbed her arms. 'I wanted this place out of my head. Max protected me here, and I should have looked after him too but I didn't, and it took him. The bad man. That fucker.'

'The Seer didn't want you here. Maybe there's something for us to find.'

Whoever built the farmhouse had done so with *rental* firmly in mind, not expending undue time or effort. To fix it now you'd start with restumping, and end by razing the lot to the ground.

More than anything else it was mournful. A family had lived here, and the house was bereft. Had been brooding on them for years.

The pebbled circular drive had almost given up and sunk into the dry weeds underfoot. Here was where a cow once stood, shoved off a trailer. Surely Lin's imagination was overcooking things but the spot appeared barren. 'We don't have to go inside if you don't want.'

'I …'

'Meaning I'm not so keen all of a sudden. Come on, let's take a stroll around the perimeter.' Beating the bounds.

Required a bit of wading through grass. High stepping like ponies. Down the left side of the property, the sinister side, an upright tin box reminiscent of a phone booth was collapsing into the weeds. Too small for a shed. Not being a country girl it took Lin two orbits to understand. '*Outside?*' Delightfully scandalised.

Carol shrugged, her uneasy grin slipping between embarrassed and defiant. 'No kid in my class had an indoors toilet. It would've been like having an elephant.'

'Yeah, an elephant you can shit in in comfort! What if you had to go at night? What about spiders?'

'It wasn't my favourite thing. Once or twice I caught Dad peeing in the sink at two am, there was a cookie in it for me if

I didn't tell Mum.'

They came to the back corner, but there was no venturing around the rear of the farmhouse. The trees crawled right up to that back wall, tangled, shoving one another, and leaned on it as though listening. *Little pigs, let me come in.*

Carol was no arborist but the grotesque lumps of banksia gave her a shudder. Her childhood had been peppered with just the tales to have her seeing faces there, leering faces, all over with lipped eyes that were also mouths.

She wished she was brave like Lin who was clambering about with her long shiny hair swinging. Something about the tall woman, her vivacity made you keen to impress her. Carol wouldn't even be here otherwise. 'What are you doing?'

'See? Over there?' With her height advantage, from an elevated mound of dirt Lin could see a charcoal cloud. She had to help Carol, wobbling, to the top and they held onto one another for balance. 'Look at us, kings of the castle. Out there. That's where the fire went through. That's what started all this for me.'

Carol gave up. Story of her life. 'I'm never going to be tall enough. And I wish it had burned this place down. I hate it.'

'Shh, the house will hear you.'

An uncertain glance to see if she was teasing.

Unable to penetrate the trees they returned to their starting point where Annie waited faithfully to carry them away. Lin had not noticed before how the farmhouse's front window gaped, boards hanging off it. Well of course there was no glass. Something had been flung through it in the dead of night, hadn't it? Waking the family. The dog had been barking.

She tried to keep her eyes off that shadowy gap in case something stirred within. 'Don't know about you but I could really go for a drink.'

No dice. Carol was already climbing the porch steps, her motion dreamy. Serve her right to put her foot through the damn thing, swanning about like that. 'I can't believe it's still here. I wonder if I'm still in there?'

'Exqueeze me?'

'Little me. From before it all went wrong.'

'I reckon it's starting to go pretty wrong right now.'

Lin vacillated before gritting her teeth and rushing after. Kate might have pondered the uncharitable *what do I owe this stranger*, but Lin was eaten up by the responsibility of bringing this young woman here. She'd known Carol didn't have all her oars in the water. 'Say, Carol, I've had this amazing idea …'

A fat shape burst from the eaves directly above their heads. Both women shrieked.

It thudded away rapidly across the boards. They barely gathered themselves in time to recognise a possum's round posterior shimmying up a tree, tail a dainty curl suspended behind that dramatic ass like a pinkie held away from a teacup.

Lin was the first to break with laughter. 'Oh my God. I think I wet my pants.'

'Did you see that?'

'What the hell do possums eat out here—people?'

'It was *all* ass! It was huge! Did it even have a head?'

'Stop it, stop or I will literally pee myself.' Wiping her eyes. 'That was a sign, right? We've had our scare, now we can skedaddle.'

Carol was emboldened. 'This was your bright idea. I want to see my old room, then we can go.'

'It's an idea I've fallen out of love with. Let's make it quick.'

No front door. It matched the no front window aesthetic, and heaven forbid any barrier exist should the house's vanished little girl wish to return. The farmhouse had been dwelling on its little girl.

They had to watch their step in the dimness of the hall. Musty carpet was laid over scoliatic floorboards but not tacked down, the edges flipped up and fraying. The walls bulged in as though to squeeze the visitors in a welcoming architecture hug. Please stay. Stay forever.

'Oh my God, wallpaper!' A decorating curiosity normally confined to England. The native climate had raised it in blisters which were not even slightly tempting to pop, in case something came worming out. Lin followed Carol's back. This was an airless, lightless, cooped-up space for a child to have crept along.

Corralled her thoughts firmly in case the hallway could hear. Friendly, friendly, we're all friends here. Just visiting. 'Which one's yours?'

She could not see her face, but Carol did not sound ok. 'Mum and Dad's room's right down the other end. Too far, if you wanted to call for help.'

'What did you say?'

'My room!' Carol sang back louder, although her back seemed to be receding at a ferocious rate without shrinking. Filling the corridor. Surely she would stick there. 'My little room. My room's this way.'

'Carol!' Lin called, staggering after. Felt like she would never catch her. Not with Carol running in great eager leaps, bounding with a child's joy through a field of warm summer grass. No beaten down adult had enough happiness to scrape together and fake that. No woman who spent her days despised for what she'd been exposed to long ago.

In the distance, a faint strangled sound. Barking? Or was that music?

'Max?' Carol laughed, her voice ringing as though to touch the sky. 'Max, here boy!' She threw open the door to her room and the concussion flung her back against the wall in the corridor.

Light poured out. Blinding light. Heat. It was like she had opened the door onto the surface of the sun. From Lin's perspective the young woman seemed to dissolve.

Fire! she thought even though it was impossible, there'd been no hint of combustion. Her emergency training insisted *you're supposed to check if the door's warm before opening it.* Well duh. Too late now.

If they wanted sane, they should have sent someone else. Lin lunged for Carol to drag her to safety, unable to see, unable to breathe. It was by lucky flailing that she managed to kick the door shut, her face smarting in the sudden dark.

The air tasted scorched. Hanging onto the smaller woman was like trying to retain an eel, Carol was twisting in her shocked grip and barking, barking, Carol was barking like a dog.

'Ms K, I couldn't see a thing when I leaped into that doorway but I felt heat flash through me, sick it felt, sick like radiation, terrible radiation of some kind.' Lin was panting, hot and dry. 'Carol, she was in front of me and her hands in front of her like she could shield her face, hide from it somehow.

'I don't even remember dragging her out of the house. Must've done it before my eyesight returned, knocking into things. Came to driving like a maniac for the emergency room with poor Carol moaning and rolling back and forth in the seat next to me with both hands still held up, rigid, the flesh coming up all raised and white. Puffing like balloons.'

Rigid with agony. Nothing hurts like burns, nothing strikes pain to the heart of you so well. And it stays. 'But Kate, I swear, there was no bedroom past that doorway. Only fire. She seared her hands—it looked like she was trying to reach through to get her dog.'

'Eric said he couldn't get through either,' Kate said slowly.

Another voice cut through the night. 'Nobody gets into the town anymore. Nobody gets out. The Seer has drawn the firestorm in a circle around it.'

Identifying the unwelcome speaker Kate jerked her torch around. Stupid! She'd been so caught up in Lin's misadventure she had missed the building hiss of *asshole incoming*.

Eyes gleamed back at her. Billy and his hounds stepped forward into the searching beam, *ha ha you found us, game over*.

'Lin! Lin, get up!' By the power of leverage Kate got the tall woman on her feet, propped against her own body, ignoring the furry unclean smell sweating out of her. Something in Kate's back pinged, promising hell later when the aggression wore off. If there was going to be a later.

She cautiously backed them up step by step. *Don't run*. The bloody avidness of the chase shone from two of those sets of eyes, urging her on. They stepped after her, drawn like magnets. Was it Kate's imagination that Billy-o in the middle spread his elbows chicken-wing style, holding them back?

'Kate.' Lin grabbed her hand, physically swivelling her attention to where they were going. 'Kate, *look*!'

The small hut poured a flickering glow into the night from every crooked seam. It sat there unburned in the char, cut off from both the town it purported to belong to and the world of mortgages and family it lured its residents from. It was impossible. The house of someone who'd truly escaped.

The door stood open, Eric having already barged in. 'But we were here!' Lin complained weakly. 'There was nothing here!'

Vindication was in no way as sweet as Kate had imagined. Listening to Billy and his cronies mutter behind them did no good either: they had obviously never seen the like. The two kids seemed gripped by fervour, Billy struggling futilely to simmer them down.

They had to step over a small kiln trench, brimming with old charcoal and ceramic shards. Shuddered to imagine the malformed little figures that had come marching out of its glow. Homunculi of unnatural influence, to be slipped into the lives of others. Many poorly made statues must have ruptured in the firing, but couldn't make an omelette without some sacrifices.

The idiot had dug the trench right before his front door and it ought to have incinerated the place, unless … unless he was already making fire his friend, even then, before the opportunity that was the great firestorm had come along.

Kate hung back until Lin gave her the stinkeye. She did not like the hut. Its smallness and shabby construction were too reminiscent of the quarantine shed. 'Keep your pants zipped Nancy Drew. We're just here to look around.'

'Are you shitting me, this is what we came for! Eric's already in there.' Bless Lin. Always wanting to be first.

The low ceiling required even Kate to duck, the interior so clumped and crowded it reminded her of a fisherman's hut. Junk dangled from hooks, she spotted cracked shoes, dolls vomiting stuffing, the limp garrotted lace of an old wedding dress. Inconsequential trinkets and albums stripped bare stacked against the walls. The photographs, in various stages of fading from view, had been used to paper the ceiling. A constellation of the left-behind up there, staring down with bleached eyes.

That took Kate aback: if you jump ship on your life, why bring any of it with you? Especially this crap. But of course anything carried in from outside the town would be treasure. And this was the abode of someone who liked to gather and keep items of power for himself. Were the residents even allowed inside to touch their memories?

There was music, as though laid on to welcome them, his special guests. The crackly orchestral strains Eric had zeroed in on came from a wind up gramophone because there was no power, and only one record from the looks of things. Music like a slow golden tide poured down the walls.

And for light, shallow saucers were placed around the single long room. Some with a strip of burning cloth for a wick, some congealed with lumpish grey tallow Kate didn't want to speculate as to the source of. It ought to have felt like a warm little space, but there was a mocking undercurrent. No wonder the Seer and Billy got on so well.

There was Eric, crouched against what passed for a wall at the far end of the narrow choked space. Given her limited options Kate snarled and hauled Lin along, sweating, feeling her heart was going to burst. Getting them clear of the doorway which was now crowded with the three firemen cutting off their escape.

Poking her way in was foxy and unpleasant. And *invasive*. A stricken beast had crawled under the porch to rot, now here came the tourists squeezing in after, laughing and taking pictures.

She almost put her foot through a wadded pile of blankets on the floor. The bed, more of a nest, was half beneath a dirty shelf and extreme contortions were required to keep cringing flesh free of the yellowed sheets, so blotchy with dried mildew and stain they looked *crispy*. Her motion disturbed the air and a deeply unpleasant funk billowed up.

However, it was clear nobody had tossed within the confines of that soiled shell for some time. Kate joined Eric, breathing hard and propping Lin against whatever part of the wall seemed clear of jagged tetanus spears. Eric looked up at them both, his eyes bruised and betrayed. 'There's nobody here.'

A cough from the doorway. His face bright with reverence Billy touched a piece of junk but seemed reluctant to enter. By accident or design his shoulders still blocked the overexcited pair who scratched and whined behind him. 'It's his. It's really his. This is the Seer's house.'

Kate mustered enough of her flagging aggression to rise, defend her last sliver of territory. 'So why isn't your precious Seer here to welcome us?'

The crackling static increased until she could scarcely catch her breath. The Seer, speaking through his chosen acolyte in a voice that was nothing but shrieking, high mindless shrieking. It drove her to her knees, down in the fust and junk.

Quivering and twitching in the current Billy almost let his dogs slip through before finding his exulted voice. 'Oh Kate. The Seer isn't among us anymore.'

It had been the most important day of his life but so much had happened Billy scarcely recalled why he'd been poking around the charred area in the first place. Hardly the locale for a pleasure stroll—following the fire it better resembled the gates of hell under a peeled sky.

Ennui, probably, the main drive of all his long baking days; it inspired a need to stride about, even pointlessly. The trouble Billy was having was a species he could not admit to. Winners did not suffer problems—that wasn't how winning worked.

The name of his trouble was Sam and Sue. A touch younger, they had been in the year below at school which was an insurmountable gulf. Now the two were subordinate to Billy at the fire station, handed over with a nod and a wink like it was all a big joke. Merely walking toward the brick building tightened the strings that tied his gut. Light hearted as mayflies, the pair had probably forgotten the day he found them in the equipment shed.

Busting a romantic interlude wouldn't have been a shock: the two had been thick as thieves since living memory, even looked alike. Billy wished it had been a discreet snog. Instead, pulling down a musty bag of wickets, Sam and Sue had exposed a shredded tissue nest with baby mice bundled at its core.

Little pinky baby mice, tiny eyes still sealed, rolling, dreaming. Exposed to the unkind air the pinkies wobbled about, questing for their mother. Perhaps they screamed for her in the peculiar hypersonics mice use to sing love songs to one another.

Their soundtrack of bright laugher, with foreheads pressed close Sue and Sam were engrossed in smashing the helpless babies with their bare hands. Even that was not especially disturbing—in the schoolyard cruelty was a way of sharpening your claws; conveniently forgotten by adults even as they benefited from the practice.

What was uncanny was how they accomplished their executions without ever looking down. They preferred to gaze fixedly into one another's eyes, perfect reflections, satisfied with the wholeness of the universe created between them.

Billy, frozen in the doorway, was the intruder, the thing from outside the universe. What was he to them? They never even bothered to look up. As he shut the door, the youthful purity of her face still bright with laughter Sue had licked pink mush from her fingers.

So far as he knew that perfect world had never cracked, never admitted a stranger. At the station Billy made sure of being a taskmaster in the hope they'd fail to recognise how tenuous his authority. His Uncle would have known what to do with the "right little bastards" but where was he? Gallivanting after his own demons, no thought to those who needed him.

Maybe that was what drew Billy to the burnt landscape: it had no conflict left. All the colour, texture and potential for harm had been blasted out of everything.

If only he could make it spread. That was what Billy wished, idly, as he walked. If only it were within his grasp to extend it to the four corners of the earth. Wasn't that he *disliked* folk, or wanted them burning—unlike some he was no psychopath. Billy was merely tired and longed for the whole mess to be wiped away.

Not everybody would have heard the wordless beckoning. Likely grim musings were in the required mix, to open him up, make him receptive to the signal he would soon become a transmitter for. It wiggled at his head as though prying a loose tooth, exposing more of the blackened underside than even Billy had suspected was there.

Prod it with his tongue-tip. Others had it too easy! That others got it all was the gall of the matter, hey? While Billy foundered in the morass of his being. Others made their errors and were forgiven with a smile, handed confidence and happiness anyhow—and see how, even that, they tossed aside and took more! If Billy's world offered no way out, why should theirs?

Thus the signal drew him in, it was like circling down the drain. Stumbling finally upon the body first shocked him, then quickly didn't. It was not the first burned person Billy had seen. He was a fireman.

At first he mistook the carbonised thing for the skeleton of a child, it had shrunk so much in the flame. The husk curled up and pitiable, abandoned out here where the land had been remade a blank slate. It seemed a miserable way to end.

How strange for it to be all alone. No buildings, no cars, no other people. Billy nudged, not it, but near it with his foot. 'Was that you calling? What do you want?'

And the buzzing rose up, which was not buzzing but a roar heard from far away, the voice of the bushfire crushing and exploding. Billy saw a sky billowing with dirty smoke, horizon to horizon. He saw his mother huddled over the bills at the kitchen table trying to weep silently. He saw cinders flung up in the air. He saw the town. He fell on his ass. He saw hands take hold of the flame and *pull.*

The fire had killed somebody. Billy ought to call it in but already knew he would not, because the charred remnant had called out to him. Had stirred something in his head. It was a relic of something powerful that had shed and left this behind amongst the char. Power being in short supply these days he was not ready to give it up just yet.

Shifting burdens single handed was rarely easy, but Billy-o was an innovator from way back. He stripped off his shirt for a reliquary to pile the bones in. Unnoticed the sun was immediately on him, its own fire too far away to do more than bite and sting, but wanting so passionately to reduce him down too.

It was when Billy touched the body that it all changed. That was when he saw where the Seer was now.

'He spoke inside my head, to *me* in a voice that was scream-ing, forever screaming. Pain's the Seer's only language now. That's how important it was to seal the town. He shed his body and hung himself on a burning hook in the sky. Gathered the firestorm, made it immortal. Drew its fury in a curtain around the town and scorched it right out of reality.

'What I saw—so bright. There's a dead spot in my vision now

in the shape of a man in the sky. These days the Seer's the only fuel the fire eats … well, unless some sad sack cretin wanders in. Looking for her doggy, maybe.'

Lin wheezed, desperate to kick his brain through his butthole but quavering limbs no longer had what it took to get her off the wall. Kate took a more diplomatic approach. 'You hid a corpse! You're going to be so fucked when we report this.' It solved the mystery of Billy's leash on his two pups: *he* found the body, and kept it from them. He was the only conduit to their screaming God.

Or at least used to be. She spoke quickly, hoping to sweep along before they twigged. 'Why are you so hot on protecting this place?'

Billy rolled his eyes theatrically, so deserving of a punch she considered throwing Lin at him. 'We're not protecting the town, Kate. *Civilisation* is. How would society and work and family hold together if there was somewhere to go? Somebody else you can be? I took up the mantle of the Seer's earthy work because any fucknut who strolls outta their life doesn't *deserve* a rathole to crawl into!'

At the climax of his grand monologue a shove sent Billy stumbling forward into the shack. And behind him those well appointed youths, well, *snarled*. Melting, blurring faces. As they stepped forward flesh dripped and sizzled on the floor. 'You and your whining and your Uncle. Always having to justify the great work. You're weak, Bill.'

'How dare you!' Billy roared, straightening. Kate winced: the slow kids always made her sad. He stabbed at them with the hand that wasn't there. 'I brought you into this, without me you've got nothing!'

Sam and Sue laughed in unison, a quick ugly ha-ha-ha that shut off fast like a couple of linked robots. 'We stand in his very house! And who brought us—not you. Outsiders!'

'You see,' the other continued—Sam? Winding a loving arm around the neck of his twin. 'We don't need you anymore, Bill. We're going to seek the Seer. It's time he knew he had new blood, *younger* blood at his service.'

'You!' Billy tried his own mocking titter, calculatedly, but his eyes flicked around in rapid little jerks searching for an escape. 'He's not going to hear *you*. You're *nothing*. You haven't even had time to be anything!'

Under other circumstances Sue and Sam might have reigned in the crazy, exerted what little control they had. But on the holy ground of the Seer's house, being shamed in front of these unbelievers—Billy had badly miscalculated.

The music jarred to an ugly, angry silence as he was thrown against the doorframe, needle ripping across the record. Grunts and scuffling that Kate did not see and didn't particularly interest her, she was already spinning away. She grabbed Lin, shoved Eric, 'Go, go, go!' Who'd have thought emergency training made for offices subdivided on the cheap would come in handy, but say it with me *a wall's not always a wall*. Kate kicked her way right through the back of the shack.

Static howling so's nobody could pretend not to hear, not even to hold those shreds of sanity together. Cringing, covering their ears as they fled. Then a held breath of pressurised silence. Eardrums popped painfully. The sensation of tipping staggered them in flight, sliding off a plate, although nobody actually tilted.

Out into darkness, not daring to turn their torches on. As far away from the hateful garbled altercation that hammered their backs as Lin could be dragged. Three blind mice they huddled behind a burnt stump Kate more careered into than found, trying to pant as softly as possible which felt next door to smothering.

'You smell that?' Kate gasped.

'Did … you … fart?' Lin seemed barely conscious. They both ignored her.

Eric nodded, coughing quietly into his fist. 'Smoke.'

Night vision grudgingly crept back as they clutched one another. It brought sheer insanity and Kate slapped both hands over her mouth to stifle expletives as shanties emerged from the dark. Ghostly things, all around, only part present and sunk to their knees in a ground hugging haze. What the three refugees found themselves huddling in was a street, or more likely an alley.

Eric rubbed his eyes, expecting normality back at every glance. His chest not big enough to contain his heart. This had to be tested. 'Ow!'

'While I admire your manly prowess, don't we have better things to do than punch walls right now?' Kate whisper-hissed.

'It can't be real!'

'You just broke your damn fingers, Eric.' Kate's nerve was getting strained, not much surplus for antics. 'And keep your voice down.'

'But Kate, this must be the town.' What there was of it. Out of nostalgia the residents had gone to the effort of laying a grid but a proper settlement would have included builders, whereas the town's siren call randomly drew the desperate, damaged and bereaved.

Construction varied pathetically. From the looks of things some arrivals had been left to cobble shelter from deadfall without a whisper of encouragement from better prepared neighbours. They had dragged themselves out here to be alone and alone they were, each locked into their private misery carried from home. The Seer's hut was practically a palace.

Kate peered through the generous gaps of one wall, then another. Nothing inside any of them, like play-houses. 'Not quite. But we're really close now. These are more like a reflection—probably left behind when the Seer firebombed the real McCoy off the planet.'

'How can you tell?'

'Well my first clue was we haven't burned to death yet.' She pointed at the stars, the broken stumps of trees, kicked the charcoal they skittered through. 'Look, the world's still here. This is just a ghost sitting on top.'

Right on cue Sam and Sue's dual voice rose in whoops. 'We're coming to find you!' As though this was some enormously fun game. Had they finished with Billy already, then? Did they lope down the streets with dripping fingers?

'Fuck. Get Lin up.' The houses were solid enough to provide a maze of cover to run through. Like a mouse fleeing, knowing it was bound to be caught. Maddening trying to pinpoint where the fierce cries rose from, sometimes left, sometimes right.

They were about to step into a cross street when Eric jerked all three back and they crouched against a wall, hearts pounding. His hearing was absolutely better. Sue galloped by on that street not three meters from where they cowered, galloped on all fours, tanned limbs flinging themselves about. The giant insect panes of her sunglasses impassive, while that running face left a viscous trail like a snail.

'Don't touch that,' Kate rasped, sudden insight. 'Don't even kick dirt over the slime when we cross. I'll bet she'll feel it and come running back.'

Eric wiped his face, breathing hard. 'This isn't working. They're going to get us.'

Lin groaned, on her hands and knees. She gagged and appeared to vomit painfully although nothing came out. 'My shoes hurt.' She was burning up. The flesh of her hands felt loose, saggy.

'So take them off,' Kate snapped.

'I can't. I'm scared my feet will come off with them.' Weeping serum tears, her life coming apart in ways she could not control.

Before she even knew she'd made the decision, as though deliberation had been done for her Kate grabbed Eric's cheeks and forced him to look at her. 'Eric! Eric, I'm going to lead them off, ok? You have to get Lin to the car. She needs a hospital.' Pressing the key into his hands.

His face crinkled. 'Why can't you do it?'

'I've already pinged my back, I can't carry her. You're not giving up on Ben here—you're being a hero. And you can come back, bring police, whatever you can get. Whatever you like. Maybe save me too.'

'Still won't work. Isn't enough cover, Kate, we can't hide …'

'Is the smoke getting thicker?' Lin wheezed. It was and it wasn't. Pale strands coiled about their ankles. The air becoming muggy, loaded with lake water.

It was seep and it was pouring from Kate as though sweating out of her very skin. Seep swaddled the town. Ran in condensation down the walls of its shabby buildings painting them with ash from the air. And the ash thickened it like clag. Visibility came down to arm's length and they huddled in fear of losing each other without saying goodbye.

Eric was done with all this. 'We're hallucinating.'

Huh. The others could see it. This was new. Almost as though drunk Kate had moved her useless dishrag ass to do something for once so they didn't have to die. She'd have to pen a thankyou card. 'Yes, you've hallucinated the perfect cover. Well done.'

He was all set to tussle so Kate sieved a damp lungful of slurry through her teeth and let rip. 'OLLY OLLY OXEN FREE!'

Appreciative screams of excitement answered from the two young idiots pelting around in the dark in sunglasses. Sue especially couldn't have got far.

'Look Eric. I know you need to find your brother, I know. But you're nothing like the other people who've ended up at the town.'

'I'm not, huh.'

'You wouldn't do anything.'

'To find Ben? I think it's clear you don't know me …'

'You're not the sort of person to let a nice girl like Lin get hurt to get what you want.'

Eric's jaw slowly hardened as he stared into her eyes. He certainly was not. And the horror was that perhaps Kate was, and he couldn't allow that. He nodded curtly with curls bobbing, jewelled with seep, and got Lin's arm hooked around his shoulders. That roused her. 'Kate,' Lin croaked ruefully. 'Think it's … pretty obvious you don't like people.'

'And here was me considering going to all this effort to save your ungrateful ass.' Lin ought to have been the adventurer, the bold, the brave. But past a certain point, all resilience leaks out with your health.

Lin attempted a smile, not all the muscles pulling. 'Stay with the train. You hear me?'

Kate brushed long hair back from her face. Still beautiful. She would be beautiful even if she died. 'I'll see you soon.'

Eric and Lin took three hobbling steps and vanished into the haze.

Kate quailed, arms wrapped around herself. Why did she do that? Being alone offered far less inspiration to be brave.

Charcoal clinked to her right. Her head snapped around and she forgot feeling sorry for herself. Hidden in the seep something was sniffing, deep congested inhalations.

'Well,' Kate whispered to herself, reaching into her handbag. 'Now seems as good a time as any for a gigantic lump of rock. Come on, now, doggy. Come on.'

A saliva-thick smacking of chops, almost right in her ear. And even as she hefted the quartz Kate suddenly saw it clearly: she could splatter one of the kids, but the last thing she would feel would be the other snatching her from behind.

Kate was smarter than this, she was certainly smarter than *them*. She needed a better plan. She ran.

Chapter Nine

Fission

Kate dashed in wild unpredictable loops through the eddying glug, swimming with her arms and hoping to get clear before the hounds zeroed in. Playing the game they could not resist. Theoretically keeping them occupied until her aching head dreamed up better; not *awesome* at running and planning, though. How long would it take Eric to reach Orphan Annie?

Pelting around a corner she collided with another warm body and almost loosed a shriek, set to brain them with her trusty rock. A hand with splayed fingers and a stump were thrust frantically in her face. 'Sh, sh, *don't!*'

It was Billy, wheezing and—oh fuckadoodledoo—covered in bites. Smeared blood described his actions of the past hour, lacking its red in the low light and crusted with ash. Obscuring how bad it was. Should Kate venture an educated guess, however, you did not give off that copper stink when things were looking up.

Her moral compass fluttered, still in favour of burying her rock between his terrified eyes and claiming she'd slipped. Sadly Billy carried no guarantee he would snuff quietly like a good boy. Sam and Sue were close. You could tell by the way their yipping had fallen silent, coursing intently between the walls somewhere out there.

'We need to get off the street.' Trying to shuffle them onto a porch. She already knew pushing the door would yield nothing, the houses sealed to deny tourists shelter; but at least they could crouch in the shadows shushing one another as they were hunted down.

Billy recoiled as though she'd beckoned him to hell. 'Not there! Haven't you heard them?'

'Clearly not.'

'Inside.' His shuddering threw off drops of blood. 'There are people shut up inside the houses.' Well that was gross.

Kate peered through the cracks again to be sure. Shadows, jumbled ash. Not even any internal walls. 'The houses are empty.'

'Not if you put your head on the wall.' A congested sob. 'I swear, they're in there. In this halfway place they whisper through the planks like ghosts.'

He was creeping her out. 'Pull your shit together and get off the damned street. I don't feel like being supper for your pals.'

Billy sniffed the tears back: if he wanted it kissed better he'd have to look elsewhere. 'Don't plan on dying, huh?' he snuffled resentfully.

'Not here, anyhow.' Keeping a sharp eye in case this was a trick Kate leaned her temple on the timber. What was that mumbling? She pressed harder into prickly splinters.

'They'll be watching for us, oh yes must be ever so foxy now.' The occupant's voice was scratchy like she'd swallowed thorns for leisure. No spring chicken. 'Pillars wouldn't let their investments just stroll off. But I'm weary from the tests, love. Can't lift my arms.'

'Hello?' Kate murmured. The certainty of a listening ear provoked another outpouring.

'A tooth fell out today. Bit into a potato and it dropped clean out, all crumbly against me gums. If you've come from the institute, you tell them if those were "vitamins" I'll be a monkey's uncle.'

'Was there a boy there with you? His name's Ben. He'd have curly hair, I think?'

'Heaps came. Pillars offered money. Not much. Electrics was too expensive, gas, you know. Me own tiny pocket not worth peanuts but the bank was coming for that, they sent a letter, all in red. Only letters I ever got was from companies, in red. I'd ask why they couldn't leave a body be but we all know that's a fool's question: the world has to keep pecking at you, pecking 'til there's nothing left.'

Kate stepped back. This was pointless. The inmate was stuck in her own gnawing injustices. It would take listening at every keyhole to find Ben, and she'd be dog food long before then. 'Sorry Eric. I tried.'

'Can we just get out of here?' Billy entreated, practically hanging off her arm.

'Oh, sure Billy, where do you want to go?' she demanded, out of patience. 'Huh? Please, I'm all ears.'

His head swivelled nervously: she was being too loud. 'I don't know, I … the light. We could go to the light. Maybe the Seer will help us.'

'Fine. Let's do that.' Probably bleed out along the way.

'Let me show you.' Quick, before she could slip beyond

reach he smeared her upper face with his own seeping fluid. Sputtering with outrage Kate skittered back, almost lost herself in the fog. She'd get pink eye for sure.

The stars cracked apart. There was a huge percussive boom and then a sustained groan, it sounded like the end of the world. Disoriented, Kate used her fingers to dig peepholes in the gore and just like that, peering through a mask of his blood she could see.

Springing up from the town's borderland a huge glistening aurora roared overhead. It lit the opaque seep so that they were suddenly drowning in a threatening orange glow that banished shadow. The stench of burning but no smoke. The only fuel those sky-high flames gobbled up was the Seer, what was left of him, and they did so ravenously.

Once that knowledge festered the wonder fell out of the spectacle, it could only be beautiful from a distance. More horrible the closer you moved. Kate wondered if the hounds could see it too, and what their teeny brains might be saying.

It appeared so. She and Billy had hardly crept ten agonising metres in this fiery new world before the dreaded shuffle and click echoed from the orange mist. Only seconds to spare— they had to crowd into another doorway as Sam came loping down the street, headed in the same direction. A shared goal, then: after catching the rabbits Sam also wanted to find the Seer.

Less playful than his twin he was not on all fours, although he trotted with the same intent focus. Sam seemed impatient, ready for the game's bloody conclusion and already preoccupied with what came next. Progress was halting as he paused periodically to the left and right, untucking from unzipped pants to mark territory. Mine, mine, mine. The hiss seemed very loud.

In the thick soup and with his glasses on Sam's next stop was opposite their hide, all unknowing. Kate pressed her sticky eyes shut with both palms. This topped the list of things she did not need to see: the young man standing amid orange eddies, hips cocked in classic pose while his face, his face behind impassive sunglasses collapsed in a swirling whirlpool.

Sam's face was sucked inward, the front of his head becoming impossibly concave like a scooped out bowel while liquid face spurted and splattered from his wagging dick. Kate bet if you disturbed one of those hidden puddles it'd bring Sam running just as quick as Sue's trail of slime.

Finally Sam shivered and shook off the last drops with a boneless flicking motion, and his face bulged and rippled back out as though suction had been released. They didn't dare move. The spreading puddle almost touched their feet.

Sam ambled off, continuing on his business and Billy risked a shuddering breath. Kate clamped his shoulder. *Not yet, this isn't finished.* Her nerves were singing.

Before the boy was entirely swallowed from view up popped Sue at her double's side like the most horrible jack in the box, jumping and wiggling with glee. Kate could feel her teeth grinding to paste. They hadn't even suspected she was nearby.

The two youths butted heads fiercely, affectionately in the middle of the street and their sunglasses clacked. They seemed to confer. Sue scrabbled at her bare arms in pantomime, she did not like the seep. When they separated Sam did so with a mock-pouty little push: fine, go then. Loped off in opposite directions to continue the hunt and the glowing seep gulped them down.

Limbs were cramping by the time Kate and Billy dared move. Or at least Billy did, stretching and twisting, grimacing to skirt the puddle. With her greater appetite for survival Kate had been pressed further in, right up against the door. She looked up at the fireman with narrowed eyes. 'This one's saying your name.'

He jumped the puddle again, squeezed in beside and put his own ear to the door. The remaining blood drained from his face and while adrenaline held him upright, it was wearing thin. 'It's my Uncle.'

This ought to be good. Kate tuned back in. A breathy old voice was droning, '… knew the town wasn't as it pretended.' You could picture him pacing back and forth in there, thinking out loud.

'Uncle?' Billy whispered as loud as he dared, tapping softly on the panel. It was like waking a tiger—the man had often struggled to sheathe irritation, even in a family setting. 'Uncle, can you hear me?'

'Billy,' the voice wheezed. 'Don't you come here.' Jealous. Possessive.

'Why did *you*?' That demand had been brewing his entire life, finally voiced. Came out more petulant than righteous but there are no do-overs.

A husky laugh. 'You're an adult now, Billy-o. Sure you're ready to get a grownup's answer instead of a kid's?'

'Just spit it out.' As assertively as he dared.

'Heard it calling me. With promises, oh, like you cannot imagine. Truth is folk got drawn here long before your "Seer" poked his snout in. The town's just some trap he went and built over the top.'

'That's crazy talk.'

'I reckon there's something else hidden in the landscape. A sort of gate. The *true* way through to where everyone's been gagging to go.'

'Not "everyone." I needed you at home. Mum needed you—how was she supposed to earn enough on her own?'

'And there's your adult answer. Everyone's their own person, Billy, chasing their own life and they'll only give four eighth's of a damn about *you* so long as it's not too inconvenient. Hate to tell you but you weren't exactly flowers and sunshine to look after. Hell, your poor mother felt it more than anyone. Wasn't any kind of job I asked for but I stuck it out for a bit.'

'"Stuck it out" —what was that, a year? You want a medal? I may not have been perfect but at least Mum did the right thing.'

Heavy breathing on the other side of the door. 'You think that was better for her? I saw what my sister went through. One night I saw her, she didn't know but I did, finally got your shit smeared ass to sleep, she tiptoed into your bedroom and held a pillow hovering above your crib. She was crying, sure, but her face was blank like a robot. Would've been so easy to press down and be free.'

Billy made a hurt noise, involuntarily, like someone kicked him. Dear old Uncle wasn't finished. 'When I finally took myself down the road and realised I didn't have to play house anymore it was like waking from a dream, my life had been a bad dream only it was over and I could be anyone.'

Billy was having trouble breathing. 'How was a … a place, a stupid *dream* more important than us?'

'It just was.'

'You fuck. You're nothing but the same selfish prick no matter how far you go. Things get tough and off you pop! Well let me share a little newsflash: there is no way through, no gate. It's just another lie you tell so you can keep being the same piece of shit no matter what.'

Defiance collapsed. The past meant nothing; this was the one topic he'd been scratching at so long there was no resistance left. 'The gate *is* here. It has to be. We can't help searching, none of us can. In case … in case it makes us better. Makes me a better man.'

Billy spat at the door. 'The Seer was right to lock you fucks away. If there's any kind of gate none of you deserve to find it.'

A whisper, like a despairing echo. 'We'll find it. We'll find it.' Muffled weeping from within.

Billy stood, wiping his eyes. 'Come on, these assholes have nothing for us. What could possibly have driven them to dance off in the first place, just magically assuming there's something nice on the other side of their fictional gate?'

'Fictional? Are you sure?' Kate was caught up in a squirming excitement she did not understand, like eels along a lake bottom.

'If, *if* the gate's even there did it occur for an instant the Seer might be protecting folk by stopping it up?'

'*Or*, and I'm just putting it out there, perhaps your Seer really is the sadistic maniac he seems to be. Someone who loves spying on people with all their hope ripped away.'

'Let's go. You'll feel differently once you've seen the light.'

The light. Somewhere out in the world dawn was spreading its slippery grey blanket, but not here. Here they were battered on all sides by the dark orange glow, like being submerged in a spill of toxic waste. It grew brighter the closer they inched to the source.

A howl from nearby. Billy winced. 'They're not going to let us leave.' And gave himself away.

Sue exploded out of the mist, grinning her dripping smile. It was like watching a child play "attack Daddy" only Billy shrieked, spinning in circles in a jittering dance. The racket was bound to draw Sam. Both tripped and tumbled over, vanishing at ground level in thick orange clag that boiled around their struggle.

On her knees groping at the mess Kate got her fingers bitten to the bone, a thumbnail torn free that she flapped frantically in the air. 'Oh you fuck-sucker!' With her good hand, coincidentally also rock-hand she flailed wildly at what was hopefully the round dome of Sue's skull; fifty-fifty, better odds than life usually offers.

Silence down there for a heartbeat which would have been the idea time to cut losses. Then Billy erupted from the tangle, eyes bulging from his head, and Kate was left to chase in his wake as he staggered down the street on the dregs of his strength.

Up ahead stood the boundary, the light, the brightness Lin had described as seen through a flung open bedroom door. Breaking free of the buildings where seep had piled up they plunged into a low lying orange sea, and sagged to a halt. The cliff face of fire blocked the way. They could approach no nearer.

Ought not to have been able to stare with retina boiled off, that's how it felt, but high in that blinding sky of all colours burning at once was a fleck that could be spotted by squinting hard enough. The famous Seer at last. The small figure shrieking its eternal death agony deserved to be seen. He'd succeeded in sealing the town, now Kate appreciated the cost and she wanted to laugh. How do you like that, fucker?

'Help us!' Billy screamed into the sky. A skittering was the only response—the only warning, coming in from left and right. Sue was for Kate now with a grudge and clamped hold before she could squirm aside, one claw gathering sheaves of hair to keep and the other digging her back as though to claim her spine. Unable to dislodge the girl Kate generously applied the rock again, and again until she fell back giving a glimpse of Sam and Billy's awkward grapple.

Fuck it. Kate whispered goodbye and pitched the rock at Sam's face. Scored dead centre, wanting to spew at the crunch it made—he wouldn't be winning world's top model now unless they had a roadkill edition.

Bleeding, on his knees Billy was still entreating the fire like a broken record. Kate grabbed him, realising in the murk she'd seized his stump when she got a handful of melted flesh. The contours of a map. At the contact the renewed signal buzzed so hard in her skull her teeth might be melting. 'Give it a rest! There's not enough left of him to hear you.'

'He's not going to help us.' Billy snivelled and she shook him mercilessly. The hounds were picking themselves up, fingertips prodding cautiously at split scalps, cracked cheekbones, pushing the damaged geometry around.

An idea hit her, brilliant and perfect. 'He was never helping anyone but himself. Us, though, we're going in.'

'What?'

'Sure, and your buddies are going to chase us. If they want to meet the Seer let's give them their chance.'

'We'll die!'

'Let's hope he recognises his bright boy.'

The roiling, blazing air tried to push back but they shoved on in, Kate towing Billy. Realising too late what was slipping through their fingers Sam snatched after them with a snarl on his face, fingertips skating off Billy's back. *Here doggy doggy.* Kate laughed hysterically. The contact spurred Billy to switch from dead weight to running. The hounds could not resist.

Billy was so slick with blood, at the change in pace Kate's grip on his stump slipped away, so quick it was like it had never been. Or did her fingers lazily open without any orders from head office? Blinded, she could not get him back. Too bad Billy. Another person who didn't save you. Guess it was down to his own demons whether he survived or not.

She recalled the map. Still fording on it was with immense satisfaction that Kate heard the pursuing hounds shriek outrage at perfect golden lives cut short. Perfect bodies and perfect viciousness. They wailed, cried out to their Seer but that speck sailing up there inhabited its own world of perfect agony and had nothing for them. They did not exist. Then they truly no longer existed, snuffed out.

It was only once the seep finished boiling off like the

inconsequential stuff it was and the exposed slimy lakebed at her core began to crack that Kate herself, both Kates began to burn and scream. But they must have known that only one Kate, by hiding behind the other, would make it across. And if one of them didn't, more fool her.

Chapter Ten

Topography

The air's always so still here. It's like nature herself tried to excise this place in revulsion.

Drunk Kate stumbled to a halt and took a short breath of the dry, over-toasted air. Brushed the flaking glaze of someone else's blood off her face in a flurry of revulsion—gross, gross, sober Kate was gross! And hell her hand hurt. Flapped at the end of her wrist like it had been through the mangle.

Eyes cleared she could finally look around, and find that without the dulling effect of the seep everything seemed too sharp. Unbearable.

Never spent much time dwelling on the blurred dual thing she had been, refused to weigh the hows and whys of coping. Well, now the fun of diving deep and letting sober Kate pick up the tab was gone. Sacrificial lamb and all that. It took a special type of broken to reach the town and sober Kate had just not been that person.

The air hung stuffy and sullen, just like in Ben's letter. Bushland crowded on all sides, where insects whirred and clicked and waited to stab. A sting on her wrist and she slapped angrily without thinking, inspected the little asterix of blood. Wasn't like bugs could make it through the fire——might have been the last of its kind. Killing the last mosquito, wouldn't that be something.

The bush concealed the true barrier. Somewhere out there, if she was tempted to retrace her steps, the fire and its madman still raged. However, rumour whispered there was a better way out. Drunk Kate intended to find it.

From ahead, in the direction of the town barking started up. At least she assumed it was a dog: the sound that carried seemed strangled, damaged. As she harried her lip and considered her options a dark cloud loomed across the landscape.

Looking up, as a tiny mote from a hill sketched on a kitchen bench, it might appear as a cloud. For an exultant moment Kate thought the towering shape had a face. It was in the name of sanity that she closed her eyes before she could recognise it.

ALSO BY BP GREGORY

Novels
Flora & Jim
The Town
Something for Everything (Automatons Book 2)
Automatons (Automatons Book 1)
Outermen

Short Story Collections
Orotund, Collected Short Stories Volume Two
Cacophony, Collected Short Stories Volume One
Vu Ja De, Collected Short Stories Volume Three

The world is frozen
The animals ascendant
And Jim will do anything
to keep his daughter alive

FLORA
& jim

BP GREGORY

The world is frozen. The animals ascendant. And, locked in desperate pursuit of the "other father" across a grim icy apocalypse, Jim will do anything to keep his daughter alive.

collected short stories
volume II

orotund

BP GREGORY

A paroled monster, a prostitute and a policeman all see a little girl lost, but this isn't the start of a joke. An isolated, frail old man trapped in his apartment; what possible threat could he pose to the sociopaths next door?

Take time for a stroll down humanity's eerie back alleys and enjoy BP Gregory's newest short science fiction, urban fantasy and horror stories neatly packaged together in Orotund: Collected Short Stories Volume Two.

BP Gregory has been an archaeology student and a dilettante of biology, psychology, and apocalypse prepping. She is the author of five novels including the recently released Flora & Jim, about a father who'll do anything to keep his daughter alive in a frozen wasteland.

BP Gregory lives in Melbourne with her husband and is currently working on The Newru Trail, a murder-mystery set in a world where houses eat your memories. For stories, reviews and recommendations as she ploughs through her to-read pile visit bpgregory.com